A Time of Hunting

A TIME OF HUNTING

Wayne Dodd

A CLARION BOOK

THE SEABURY PRESS

NEW YORK

Library of Congress Cataloging in Publication Data

Dodd, Wayne, 1930-
A time of hunting.

"A Clarion book."
SUMMARY: Glimpses an adolescent's change of values and
perceptions during Depression days in Oklahoma, especially
regarding hunting, his only way of earning money.
[1. Depression—1929—Fiction. 2. Hunting—
Fiction]
I. Title.
PZ7.D6628Ti   [Fic]   75-4779
ISBN0-8164-3151-5

A Time of Hunting

·1

Queenie loved to hunt better than anyone or anything I've ever seen. Give her a little encouragement and I think she'd have hunted until she dropped dead.

The first time I really got interested in hunting was because of Queenie. I heard her barking one Saturday afternoon in what we called the vacant lot, across the road from our house, though it was really more of a field than a lot. Well, she was barking and barking, so finally I went to see what it was all about. And there she was, with her head up to her shoulders in a hole in the ground, her hind legs braced like she was getting set to drive through to China.

She was so eager and excited she didn't even notice that I was there. First she would sniff long and slow, like someone trying hard to identify a smell, and then she'd snort real sharp and bring her head up out of the hole. Then she would start digging with her front paws, just as fast as they would go, with her ears laid back alongside her head and a deep, knowing look in her eyes. All the time she was digging she would be whining and fretting, so that you just knew she was so close to whatever it was that she simply couldn't wait to get at it.

So I started getting pretty excited too. I bent over and pulled away some of the loose dirt Queenie had scratched up and tried to look in the hole. But it was dark and black, and besides, this caused Queenie to go into a frenzy of digging and whining. I thought it was clear that we were about to catch the animal, whatever it was, so I ran back to our house and got a shovel to help dig. But every time I dug a little, trying to follow the tunnel and get a little bit ahead on it, there was Queenie's nose, sniffing and snorting like she was having an attack of asthma.

She stayed in that state of excitement all afternoon and all across that field. Dad came out once, about four o'clock, and said I was just egging her on by getting involved in the digging. He must have been interested, though, because he stayed and helped, the three of us encouraging one another and taking turns digging right up till supper. When one of us was digging, the other one had to hold Queenie. Otherwise she'd be up to her shoulders in the hole again, sniffing and snorting as she tested the scent, right in the way of the digger.

Along about twilight we finally got to them, a den of civet cats, three of them. I had to stay back a little ways from the hole right at the last, to keep Queenie from grabbing one of them. We could expect to get up to $5.00 apiece for those hides, and of course Queenie would have torn the fur and probably ruined it if she got ahold of one. Also, Dad said we didn't want her getting hit with that smell or we'd never be able to stand her around the house again.

Dad had gone back to the house and got his rifle, though he said he probably wouldn't have to shoot one. He had brought a flashlight too, which he could shine in the hole to see what was in there.

From where I was I couldn't see very well what happened, but Dad made some quick movements and I could hear the sound of something hitting the shovel hard. All of a sudden one of the civet cats broke away and dashed across the open field, with only its white V stripe down its back showing clearly in the dusk. I was so surprised that I must have relaxed my grip on Queenie's collar, for she tore after it with a snarl and a whine, and I started out right after her, just as fast as I could go. But the ground was uneven and pretty cloddy, so that wasn't very fast.

Later Dad said maybe that was just as well.

At least I wasn't close enough when it happened to get hit too. Of course, Queenie caught the civet cat before it got more than halfway across the field. But in all her years of hunting, Queenie had never faced a skunk or civet cat out in the open like that. She wasn't cagey or tricky or anything. She just ran straight at it, and though I couldn't really see, I heard when it happened. The civet cat must have turned and squirted her right square in the face with its scent, then turned and ran toward the woods.

Queenie yelped like she had been shot, and by the time I got to her she was rolling on the ground, rooting in the dirt with her muzzle, trying to get the feeling off. Naturally the smell was awful, but Dad said that it wasn't just the smell that was hurting her. He said the musk was probably burning her nose and eyes pretty bad.

Dad carried the two civet cats home while I stayed and rubbed dirt from the hole all over Queenie's coat. It was supposed to take some of the smell off, but I don't think it helped any. Or at least not much. I didn't do it for long because Queenie was so sick to her stomach I just couldn't bear to make her stay out there. I took her home and left her in the garage. I could hear her heaving and vomiting all the way to the back door of the house.

The next morning we had to skin the civet cats and start to dress the hides out beside the garage. Dad helped me do it, though he said that after we got the skins on the boards the job was all mine.

In the sunlight the civets looked beautiful. The fur was coal black, with the absolutely snow-white stripes running along each side of the back until they came together at the base of the head and then ran over the forehead and to a point just back of the nose. The fur was soft and glistened in the sunlight, almost like it was wet. They looked as if they were asleep, except for the trace of dirt in the nostrils. And their feet were tiny and black and helpless-looking.

Dad skinned them. He made a slit down the inside of each hind leg, from the base of the tail to the foot, and then one around the bottom of each leg just above the foot. Then he peeled the skin off, pulling it over the civet cat's head and turning it inside out as it went. He peeled it off real slow, so as not to tear a hole in the fur and ruin it. As he pulled, he pared it away, with a knife, from the sheath of fat that surrounds the animal. Finally it came right off the end of the nose, with all the fur on the inside of the hide.

Then we slipped the hides onto the curing boards that Dad and my brother had made years before. The boards were flat and scraped as smooth as glass, and they tapered to a round point at one end. They were square at the other. We fastened the nose of the hide to the tip of the board with a tack, and pulled the hide down until it was stretched nice and taut. Then we tacked down the hind legs of the skin. After that the only thing to do was to scrape the remaining fat off the hide. You did that over a period of several days, as the skin dried and the sun warmed the fat and made it soft and easy to scrape off.

It was really pretty interesting work once the skinning was done. And then too, the tip of the skin didn't look quite so much like a nose once it was on the board.

I sold those two hides for nine dollars and a half when they were completely dried. I was pretty well hooked after that.

But Queenie never did get over that affair with the civet cats. She got over the sickness, and her eyes quit being all red and swollen after a few days, but her nose never was so sensitive afterwards, not as it had been. Dad said he wouldn't be surprised if our own noses had been permanently injured too, by having to smell Queenie for the next two weeks or so. We all laughed about that.

But it was true that after Queenie got hit with the civet cat scent she had trouble sorting out trails when we went hunting. And after all, that's what makes a good hunting dog, being able to pick the warmest trail from all the ones it comes across. Otherwise, it would just wander around smelling the old trails of animals in the woods and never get anywhere. And that's just what we did a lot of the time. Oh, Queenie hunted just as eagerly as ever. And when you got into the woods with her, it was still exciting to hear her suddenly bay out with her big voice through the night. And sometimes she would "tree" as well as you could hope. (I guess that's when she struck a trail that was so warm she just couldn't get it mixed up with old trails that crossed it.)

But many times we could tell by hearing her that she was uncertain, or had lost the trail and was looking for it, circling around and around, hoping to strike it again (for she was still a smart hunter, as smart as any hunting dog you'd hope to see). Sometimes she'd even end up coming back to us where we were standing in the dark, waiting for her to find the direction. She'd be confused and embarrassed, because this wasn't what she had been used to.

So I really wasn't surprised when Dad read me the ad one night. "Year-and-a-half-old male Black-and-Tan trained coon hound. Will not chase rabbits. Also good possum dog.

Guaranteed. $50.00. Shipped from Paducah, McCracken County, Kentucky, heart of the South's coon country."

Dad was looking at the ads in the back of a *Field And Stream* magazine he had borrowed from Jack Patton, the barber. I was just sort of fooling around in the living room when he said this, and Mother was sitting on the other side of the room, sewing a patch on the back of Dad's old jacket.

"Sounds good to me, Jess," Dad said. "What do you think? He's guaranteed. If he's no good, we can send him back and won't cost us nothing but the return freight. Says three weeks' trial period."

I couldn't help glancing over at Mother, and I saw that she had looked up too. She looked at Dad for a minute but didn't say anything. Then she looked back down at the jacket.

Dad was a truck driver, and he wore this jacket that didn't have any back left to it. The back had completely worn away from sitting in the truck so much and bouncing up and down on rough roads. He still wore it because he said we couldn't afford a new one, which was probably true. It was 1937, right in the middle of the Depression, and we didn't have much money. Anyway, Mother had patched that coat I don't know how many times, and she had used some sort of heavy black cotton cloth for the patching. The coat itself was a medium blue check, made out of wool, so the back looked like the back from a completely different coat. And now even some of the patches were beginning to wear out. Well, announcers were always reading things over the radio that people had written about their products, and it was a joke at our house that every time one of them would say "unquote" at the end of what he was reading, Dad, or one of us, would say something like, "Did he say 'uncoat' just now? Say, I sure wish they'd send that coat they keep taking off those guys along this way." And Dad would show us the back of his old jacket, turning slowly around a couple of times like a model. Mother would laugh till she got tears in her eyes. I laughed a lot too.

But now Mother just sat there and kept sewing on the jacket. Dad didn't look her way. He just kept looking at the magazine in his lap. "Yes, sir," he said. "A Black-and-Tan coon hound."

That's what Queenie was too, a Black-and-Tan. And she'd been a fine hunting dog for a long time. When my brother was still at home, he and Dad had caught more coons with Queenie than just about anyone else in the county. But as I said, her nose wasn't much good now, especially on a cold night. And hunting season is in the winter.

So I looked down at a piece of string I had in my hands and said, "Yeah, he sounds real good, like just what we want. But $50.00 sure is a lot of money." I stole a look at Mother out of the corner of my eye. She didn't look up, but I noticed she had stopped sewing.

"Well, we can try it," Dad said. "If the dog's any good, we can more than pay for it in hides in just one season easy. Paducah, Kentucky! I'll bet that's a real fine dog."

I couldn't believe it. $50.00 for a dog! I was afraid that any minute now Dad would laugh and say it was all a joke.

He looked up at me and grinned. "They say it'll take ten days," he said. "We'll send for him in the morning."

I was so excited I could hardly stand it. Paducah, Kentucky! McCracken County! A pure-bred Black-and-Tan!

Dad put down the magazine sort of casual like and stood up. "We'll probably get more hides than we'll have time to stretch," he said. "Then just watch my old blue jacket, eh Jess? Testimony from another satisfied customer. Coat, uncoat." and he looked at Mother.

She smiled some, but not very much.

·2

Next day I went downtown to mail the letter ordering the new dog. I saw Toby's truck over at the old Masonic Hall and ran home as fast as I could to tell Mother.

Since there wasn't any regular movie theater in our town, Toby would bring his equipment around from time to time, rent the downstairs of the Masonic Hall for a week or so, and show a different movie every night. He did this in small towns all around the area. Toby had a pretty large family, about five or six kids, and I think he just barely made a living. But he was a nice guy, kind of tall and gangly, and he had a very big Adam's apple. Once, a couple of years before, I stayed to help fold up the chairs and put them in his truck after the last night's movie. When we finished, Toby got each of the other three guys to give up a nickel apiece of the quarter he had promised them. I don't think they liked it too much, although they still got five cents apiece more than I did, and as

Toby pointed out, I worked as hard as any of them.

When I got home, Mother was scrubbing the kitchen floor. She asked me if I had mailed the letter to Kentucky, and I told her I had. I said I bet it would be the best coon dog in the whole state. Unquote. But she didn't smile much.

"He better be," she said, "for that kind of money."

"You don't seem to be very interested in us getting a new dog," I said.

"It's not that I don't want you and your dad to get another dog, Jess. It's just that we can't afford to be paying out $50.00 for one, especially some dog that we've never even seen before."

"Yeah, but this one's going to make money for us," I said. "It's a trained coon dog, and guaranteed."

She brushed some hair back out of her eyes and said, "Well, I don't think we'll rush right out and buy anything on credit with all that money he's going to make."

There didn't seem to be anything to say in answer to that, so I just sat there watching her for a few minutes.

Then after a while I told her about Toby.

"Yes, I guess it's about time for him to be around again," she said.

"I was wondering whether you thought I

might be able to go to the movie some while he's in town," I said. "I'd sure like to go once or twice."

She didn't answer at first, just went on scrubbing and sort of pursing up her lips. So I started to get worried.

Then after a little while she said she thought maybe we could arrange it so I could go every night. And she looked real pleased at the thought.

"Why don't you go down and ask Toby if he would take a peck of potatoes every night in exchange for letting you see the shows?" she said. "We've got more potatoes than we'll be able to use this winter anyway. Some of them will probably be going to rot before summer as it is."

She smiled and wiped her hands on her apron. "So you go ask Toby."

Naturally I was delighted when she said I could go every night, almost as surprised as when Dad decided to pay $50.00 for the new dog. But the talk of the potatoes sort of took the edge off it. For some reason I just didn't want to ask Toby to trade. I really didn't know why. As Mother said, Toby would probably be glad to get them—good white potatoes, right out of our own garden.

"Nothing wrong with that," she said.

I said I guessed not and then went out and

practiced sticking an ice pick in the side of the garage. Throwing underhanded I could make it stick better than I could throwing overhanded, but I missed a lot that way too.

After a while I went back downtown to talk to Toby.

When I got there, there were already quite a few kids standing around watching Toby work. So I watched for a little while too.

We were all on the porch watching Toby get his projector set up, when along came Jim Fannin's sister Billie Jean and their cousin Imogene Ridley. Imogene was fourteen, same age as I was, and she lived on a ranch near a town called Crowfoot, about twenty miles away. She came to visit Jim and Billie Jean pretty often because she and Billie Jean were about the same age and I guess they liked each other quite a bit. Imogene had very dark shiny hair and beautiful long eyelashes. She was a very pretty girl, and I had talked to her some at basketball games and places like that.

Well, Imogene came up to me and said she hoped she would see me at the movie tonight. I said yes, I was coming. She smiled and said good and then walked over to where Toby was now selling tickets for the first night's performance.

"Aren't you going to get your ticket?" she asked.

I looked at her hair and then down at the wooden porch. The cracks between the boards were filled level to the top with dirt. I squatted down and dug at the dirt with a nail I had in my pocket.

"No," I said. "I'll get it tonight."

Somehow I just couldn't ask Toby then, not in front of everyone—especially Imogene. I didn't know what it was, but my face felt all hot and flushed. The fact is, I was embarrassed to offer to trade Toby the potatoes.

Once the summer before I had felt the same thing. I was working on a farm near town (which I always did in the summer since we needed the money) and along came Billie Jean and Imogene on saddle horses from Imogene's ranch. I was standing in the shade of the hay wagon, drinking from the water jug and smelling the damp, musty smell of the wet gunny sack that was wrapped around the jug to keep the water cool. I looked up and there they were, about fifty yards away and even with the wagon. I could see how pretty Imogene was even from there. She had on a violet-colored blouse. I saw her starting to wave just as my eyes came level with them over the water jug. And suddenly I turned away and did something with the wagon, seeming to be busy. I pretended not to see her. I didn't know why I did it. They still saw me, of course. So it was a silly thing to do. But I guess I was ashamed of being poor and having to work like that while they were out riding horses.

Now I turned around and walked off the porch of the Masonic Hall. I felt strange and couldn't even see clearly. I would ask Toby tonight, I thought.

I didn't like being ashamed of being poor. So I shouted over to a group of men on the sidewalk across the street that we were going to get a thoroughbred hunting dog. "He's costing us $50.00," I said.

One of the men was Imogene's uncle, Cecil Clelland, who was always making jokes to me and everyone else.

"Hey, Jess," he said. "Is it true that you still slumber in the bed?" And he almost fell down laughing, just as if he had said something really funny. All the other men laughed too. I glanced across the street and saw Imogene still on the porch. She was laughing too.

That night I didn't go to the movie. I went downtown all right, and over to the Hall. But when I got there Toby was busy, and there were so many people around I just couldn't see any way I could make the potato proposition. So I just fooled around out front with all the other people, and when they went in to get seats, I sort of stepped around the side of the building and stood there in the dark.

Later I could hear the sounds of the movie inside.

I thought about Imogene. She had on a light yellow blouse tonight and a sort of pink-and-gray checked jacket. I thought she looked beautiful. I wondered if she would want me to sit by her if I was inside.

I also thought about the new hunting dog and the hides I would get with him. No more standing around outside the Masonic Hall then, I said to myself. And no more potatoes either. I'd probably take Imogene to get a coke or a milk shake some Saturday and maybe buy her a hamburger at the next basketball game. We might even go horseback riding together. I figured that with Queenie to help get him started the new dog would be hunting well for us in no time. And of course the ad said he was a coon dog. So we would probably start catching more coons and less possums. A good, well-dressed possum hide was worth maybe seventy-five cents or a dollar. Maybe even a dollar and a quarter. A coon skin would bring anywhere from $10.00 to $15.00.

It was quite dark outside, and I could see the stars clearly. I sat on the ground and looked at the big dipper and then turned and looked for the little dipper until I found it. I had seen them often enough when we were hunting. I listened to the sounds of the movie and thought about hunting and about listening to the sounds of Queenie on the trail and about Imogene's shiny black hair, long and as soft-looking as a fine fur.

It was sort of strange the way it happened. I was thinking of her hair like that, and suddenly there she stood in front of me, with Billie Jean just behind her.

"I thought you must have come outside," she said. "We couldn't see you inside anywhere."

I was so startled I couldn't think of any way to explain what I was doing. So I lied about it. "It seemed stuffy inside."

"I had hoped you would sit beside me," she said. "We don't get to see each other very often."

"I couldn't see where you were sitting," I said, which in a way was true.

"Now it's too late," she said. "There was an empty seat next to me before the show started. But now there isn't one."

I was thankful it was dark, so she couldn't see how relieved I was. "That's too bad."

Imogene nodded.

"Imogene's going to come and stay with me during the invitational basketball tournament next month," Billie Jean said. "Maybe you can go to some of the games with us."

I think Imogene was smiling. I know I was. I tried to swallow some of my excitement.

"I would like that very much," I said.

Then she said something that again made me glad it was dark.

"Do you like me very much?" she asked. Just like that she asked me, looking me right in the face as she said it.

I stood there looking at her, and she looked so beautiful I could hardly breathe. I nodded my head yes.

She smiled then and said we should write letters to each other. That way we would be closer.

I had a Barlow pocket knife in my hand, which I had been fiddling with while we talked. The blades were closed.

Suddenly she took the knife from my hand and put it to her lips and kissed the handle.

"Now you kiss it too," she said.

And I did.

Somehow she reminded me of the stars just then, so I almost told her about the new dog and all. But I didn't.

Then she said they had to get back inside, and they both left.

I stood there a few minutes thinking about what she'd said. Then I put my knife in my pocket and walked home. I still didn't say anything to Toby about the potatoes.

·3

The next week went by very slow. I marked the days on the calendar when I came home from school, and first thing in the morning on Saturday and Sunday. I really couldn't think much about anything except the dog.

At night I would talk with Dad about it.

"What do you think he'll be like?" I'd say.

"Well," he would say. "He's just a year and a half old, so I'd guess that he'll be plenty lively. Probably still a little bit puppyish in some ways, though old enough to have some pride and character too. Yes, he ought to be a pretty good one." And he would rub his legs and smile with pleasure at the thought.

"Of course, he's already trained," I'd say. "So he should be ready to get started right away."

"Yes, I suspect he'll be the best hunter we've seen since Queenie was in her prime."

Mother never did join in much in these conversations, although from time to time she would act sort of impatient when we talked about the new dog too long.

Then she would say something like, "This is a lot of foolishness and I think you both know it. Paying half a month's salary for a dog is not going to do anything to keep us off the soup lines, even if it is a trained coon hound."

"We're not on the soup line yet," Dad would say. "And we're not about to be, either, not while I still have a regular job."

"No, but a lot of people are these days, and we're not all that far from it ourselves. Why, you don't even have a decent work coat to wear. And we can't afford to buy you a new one."

"Unquote," Dad would say, and wink at me and pick up a newspaper.

Then I would get a book or something too. But I always had a hard time concentrating on what I was reading.

Sometimes, to keep my mind off the dog, I would think of Imogene. One night when I was thinking of her, I thought of the first time I had ever noticed her much. It was about a year and a half before, just before school was out for the summer, and a bunch of us from the same class went on a picnic in the woods outside of town. Two teachers went along as chaperones. Imogene's school was out or something and she was visiting Billie Jean, so she came along too.

Everyone brought a picnic lunch, and we put them all together to make one big lunch that we all shared. We had a good time, sitting around on the grass, about twenty-five of us, eating and laughing and joking.

I had never really thought about how pretty Imogene was before. I guess I had never even noticed. But I noticed that day. And others did too. Every time she smiled, all of the guys would act sort of silly. There was a lot of showing off.

After lunch someone asked if we could go swimming in the creek. But no one had brought a bathing suit along. The teachers talked it over for a few minutes and finally decided that it would be all right for us to swim in our underwear if we wanted to, since our underwear would cover us up about as well as bathing suits.

We were all self-conscious at first, and everyone sort of halfway hid behind a tree while taking off their clothes.

Pretty soon, though, quite a few kids were in the water, which was still cold, so more and more started going in.

We were all about the same age then, about twelve or thirteen years old, but some were more developed than others, especially the girls. And once the underwear was wet the differences were more obvious. I noticed once when Imogene got out on the bank to jump into the water that she looked like a teenager.

I think the teachers were a little bit surprised at how mature Imogene and some of the other girls were. Anyway, I felt pretty funny about it, and for a while I just stayed in the water and wouldn't get out on the bank to jump in, even though some of the kids called to me and asked me to.

Then after a while I got a boy named Benny Martin to go with me, and we both got out of the creek and went a roundabout way back to the picnic spot. We each took a small orange left from lunch and put it inside our shorts, to make them bulge out in front. Then we circled around again and came back to the creek. I felt dumb while I was doing it, but I did it anyway. Some of the guys snickered when we waded into the water, and even some of the girls did too. I couldn't help noticing Imogene, but she was looking in another direction right then.

Once we were back at the creek and in the water, there didn't seem to be anything further to do, so we just stood around in the water up to our waist, feeling silly and probably looking it too.

It was all a little stupid, and I guess maybe the teachers were embarrassed or something, because shortly after that they said we would all have to get out.

Now I sat there wondering what Imogene

had thought about all that. I knew the girls had talked about it some on the way home, so she must have known. But she never gave any sign.

I hoped she didn't still remember.

It was kind of a funny thing, but when I started thinking of Imogene, I would forget about the dog for a while. And then I would begin to want to see Imogene too. Sometimes I couldn't tell which one I wanted to see most.

·4

The new dog finally came on Wednesday, eight days after we ordered him. We went down to the train station to get him in Dad's car. But we took the back seat out first to make room for him.

I was surprised when I saw him. He was in kind of a large cage with a wooden floor, and wire around all the sides and across the top. There was a little bit of straw in the bottom of it and an empty bowl in one corner. The straw was wet around the bowl, so I guess it hadn't been too long since he'd had some water.

But he looked pretty bad. He was dirty and smelly from being cooped up in that cage for several days, and on top of it all he looked half sick. He had his tail tucked between his legs as though he had been whipped, and I could see most of his ribs showing through his skin. Dad said he looked like he hadn't been fed for a week, and that was probably so.

His name was printed on a metal tag on the side of the cage. It was "Duke."

We took him home before we uncaged him. We wanted to have Queenie around when we took him out to help him feel more at home. Besides, he was too dirty to ride in the car outside of the cage, even with the back seat out.

On the way home Dad said it was to be expected that the dog would be somewhat cowed after a trip like that, and that some good food and a bath would probably perk him up a lot.

I began to feel better about him then.

I admit I was a little disappointed at first. It had been a long week of waiting, and I hadn't exactly pictured him like that, all tired and trainsick and weak. I thought that for $50.00 you ought to get a fine, purebred dog, and I expected him to look like one. Of course, I hadn't thought any about how he would come, or how all of this might seem to him. I had been thinking a good bit about Imogene and about how we had kissed my knife and about how much money I would make from the sale of hides with the new dog.

I hadn't seen Imogene since the night at Toby's, for when I finally did go to the movie two nights later, she had already gone back home. I saw Billie Jean there, but we didn't talk much. I didn't bother to ask Toby about a trade for the rest of the nights. I brought him the potatoes for that one night the next morning.

Dad said the dog appeared to have real good markings, like a first-class Black-and-Tan. He said the long ears were a good sign. And I thought his name sounded fine for a trained hunting dog. Duke.

When we got him home and unloaded, Queenie became very excited. She sniffed and bounced around while we were uncrating him, so we could hardly work. It was almost like the time we were digging out the civet cats.

I guess Duke was glad to get out of the cage, but he didn't show it. He just stood around and quivered and tucked his tail between his legs when Queenie tried to sniff him.

Dad said he was probably scared and worn out.

While we were standing around watching Duke and Queenie getting acquainted, Cecil Clelland came driving past our house and saw us. He stopped the car and got out and walked over to the fence.

"Got the new dog, eh?" he said. He had a toothpick sticking out of the corner of his mouth. I don't know why, it wasn't even lunch time yet, and it was long past breakfast.

"That's him" Dad said. "Name's Duke."

"Well, now, that's a pretty rich name," Cecil Clelland said, "for such a poor-looking dog." And he started to laugh, without even taking the toothpick out of his mouth.

"Yes, sir," he said, "that's a pretty poor-looking dog. I don't think I'd care to have him on my hands. No siree."

"He looks pretty hard after the train trip," Dad said. "We'll have to feed him up and put some meat on his bones." He leaned over and patted Duke on the side, and you could hear his hand against the bones underneath the skin. Duke just stood there with his tail and head both hanging down and his back humped up in the middle.

"Sure doesn't seem to have much spirit in him, does he?" Cecil Clelland said.

"No, but we just got him out of the cage," Dad said. "He'll come around in a few days." And he started scratching Duke's back. Queenie came over and nuzzled Duke on the neck.

"I sure wouldn't want to buy how much food it'll take to fatten that skinny creature up," Cecil Clelland said, and he pointed at Duke with his toothpick as he said this.

Dad had been half smiling while they were talking, but now he stopped smiling and stood up suddenly. "I don't think you need to worry any about that," he said. "I don't remember offering to sell him to you."

Cecil Clelland looked up at Dad, a sort of surprised expression on his face. He was still leaning over with his arms resting on top of the fence. Then he smiled again.

"That's right," he said. "I don't guess you did."

Dad still didn't smile, though. So Cecil Clelland took his arms off the fence and straightened up.

"Well, I'll be seeing you," he said, as he turned away.

He walked over and opened the door of his car. Then he looked back and took the toothpick out of his mouth. "Yep, like you said, Jess, he's a thoroughbred right enough. You can tell that just by looking at him." He laughed and got into the car and drove off.

Mother came out about then and stood looking at Duke with her arms folded.

"So that's the new hunting dog, is it?"

She didn't seem very excited.

"Yes, ma'am" I said. "That's Duke, a thoroughbred Black-and-Tan coon hound, from McCracken County, Kentucky. Guaranteed." I decided not to say "Quote, unquote."

"Sure doesn't look like much of a dog to me," she said.

"We're not getting him to show," Dad said. He sounded angry. "You don't judge a hunting dog by how he looks but by how he hunts."

I thought that was a pretty good point.

·5

Naturally we couldn't wait to take Duke hunting. Dad said we really ought to give him a few days to rest up and get used to us before taking him out, but by Saturday we were just as jumpy as frogs. We simply couldn't wait any longer.

Anyway, Duke seemed to have settled down pretty nicely already. He had been eating well and had slept a lot. And of course, Queenie had helped too. Queenie was a real solid, stable kind of dog. She could get as excited about hunting as any dog could, but she wasn't nervous or flighty or anything like that. So she helped settle him down. We could tell right away that he liked having Queenie to depend on.

We decided to take him out on Saturday night, not for a long hunt, but enough to break him in a bit and to give us some idea of what he was like. We probably should have taken him out first in the daytime, since he was new to us and all, but we didn't. After all, the best hunting is at night. That's when the animals do most of their own hunting and traveling, so there are more trails for the dogs to strike.

We got our stuff ready before supper, and as soon as it was dark we left. When we stepped out into the yard, I thought we got our first good sign. Queenie always started getting excited the minute she saw us come out of the house with rifles and flashlights, and she started in now just as usual.

Duke started too. All day Saturday he had just loafed around, without showing very much life at all. Now he was barking like crazy. It was easy to see that he liked to hunt. And I thought he had a good, clear-sounding voice. We would be able to hear it for a long way when he was on a trail.

They quieted down some in the car, but you could still feel their excitement. Queenie whined quietly from time to time, as she always did at times like this. We were taking her along because she always helped to get a hunt started fast. She might not be able to stick with the trail every time now, but she could be counted on to strike a trail early. Also she would be a help in getting Duke back to us and the car when we were ready to go home.

The dogs lit out just as soon as we opened the car door. They were out of sight in the woods almost as soon as they started.

It was a good night for a hunt. The air was cold and dry, and the moon was almost full. The trees were dark and clear in the moonlight, so we could see where we were going without the flashlights. We could see our breath just as clear as under a street light. Everything was very still. Dad snapped a dead branch off a tree and it sounded as loud as a rifle shot.

Sure enough, Queenie was the first to strike a trail. We heard her big clear voice over to one side of us and moving away. We didn't say anything; we just started following her call. It felt good to be walking. There was no wind, so as long as you were moving you stayed warm.

Pretty soon we heard Duke too, and in a couple of minutes we could tell that he had joined Queenie on the trail.

It's exciting when a dog first strikes a trail. You're walking along and it's so quiet you can hear the breathing of the person with you. Then the dog bays out loud and excited like, and everything is changed. Your heart really does seem to beat a little bit faster.

But if it turns out to be a pretty long trail, with the dogs baying and running and you listening and following, it gets to be sort of boring after a while. Of course, we wanted to know how well Duke could stick to a trail and whether he was a good enough hunter to either tree what he was after or give up and go on to a better trail. So I guess it took longer than usual for us to start getting bored.

But it finally became clear to both of us that the dogs weren't getting anywhere with this one. Their baying wasn't moving in any single direction now.

We sat down on a fallen tree and listened for a few minutes. We had heard Queenie like this before. I sometimes thought she was baying just to give herself encouragement. I pulled a piece of bark off the dead tree and crumbled some of it in my fingers. I looked at Dad. In the moonlight the side of his face next to me was light and clear. The other side was dark and out of sight.

"Sounds to me like they're just making a lot of noise and hoping," he said.

I thought so too, though I didn't want to. They were both still baying fairly strong—not like dogs that have a hot, fresh scent, but not like they'd lost it either. So I still had some hope.

But it didn't last long. Pretty soon we could tell that Queenie didn't really have a clear trail anymore, and we could also tell that Duke was just echoing her call and not actually saying anything on his own.

It didn't sound too hopeful.

"Doesn't seem to know when he's on a good

trail and when he's not," Dad said. "We might as well call 'em in for tonight."

"I guess so," I said. He had already started calling them, so I doubt if he heard me.

They caught up with us before we got to the car, Duke seeming just as pleased as punch with himself, though I couldn't see why. I guess he had simply enjoyed the hunt. He trotted quietly along behind Queenie the rest of the way to the car.

Dad was awful quiet. I was glad that Imogene couldn't see us now.

The dogs hopped into the back seat of the car as soon as I opened the door. Duke sat up real straight on the seat, with his long tongue hanging down to one side.

Dad looked over at him as he got in behind the wheel. "A purebred back-of-the-sedan coon hound," he said. His grin was sort of lopsided.

· 6

That's pretty much how it went after that. We kept taking Duke out, hoping that this time he would prove to be a well-trained hunting dog, but he never did. Now and then he would show real promise, but it was only that—promise. One specially good night he led the treeing of two possums and even made a good run on what we thought must be a coon trail, but Queenie never did seem to pick it up for sure, and Duke ended up losing it after a while. Something went wrong every time.

Once we took Duke out by himself to see what he could do without any help from Queenie. That was two weeks after we got him. We never did hear from him after we went into the woods.

At first, of course, we didn't think anything about it. We thought he was ranging around, waiting to strike a scent, the way dogs do. After about half an hour we started to wonder. Finally we called to him, first Dad and then me. We whistled and hollered, but he didn't bark or anything. So we stood there in the cold and waited, every once in a while whistling or calling to him.

After about an hour Dad said we should go back to the car and sound the car horn, maybe that would get him to come. He was plainly worried.

As we walked back to the car, Dad pointed out that Duke was still new to the area and might have gone too far to hear us and couldn't find his way back. He said he guessed we should have brought Queenie.

When we got to the car, Dad opened the front door on the driver's side and turned on the headlights. Then he honked the horn. I was standing over to one side, listening for any kind of sound from Duke. I was looking down toward the ground, not really looking *at* anything, and suddenly there came Duke, crawling out from under the car, right behind Dad. He humped his back up, so that you could see his backbone, and then stretched and yawned, just as Dad turned around and saw him.

I guess it could have been a pretty funny sight. Cecil Clelland laughed all over the barber shop when I mentioned it a few days later. He said that dog sure did seem to be the fly's thighs all right and slapped the barber on the back. The barber stopped cutting my hair for a minute or two while he polished his glasses.

But Dad didn't think it was funny. He said that this was the last straw and that he was sending that dog right back to where it came from.

We were both quiet on the way home.

I was hoping Dad would change his mind. But he didn't. Mother said that of course he was right to send the dog back.

"We can't pay $50.00 for a dog that can't even find the woods by himself," she said.

So Dad said we would send him back tomorrow.

I felt very bad about it. I had to admit that Duke hadn't proved to be much of a hunting dog, but I sure didn't like to think of sending him back. We had all gotten used to him, and I knew that Queenie would be lonesome without him.

So I tried again to change Dad's mind, just before I went to bed.

"Don't you think we could try him one more time?" I said. "We could still send him back after that—if he didn't do any better."

Dad shook his head. "He's just not a trained hunting dog, Jess. And that's what we were paying for. I admit that he could probably be trained to be a good hunter, but I haven't got the time to train him. And we can't pay $50.00 for him just as a companion for Queenie. We just can't do it."

No one said anything for about a minute. You could hear the clock ticking on the mantel.

Finally Dad said, "I'm sorry, Jess. I wanted him to be a good hunting dog just as much as you do. But he's not. And every day he stays with us will make it just that much harder to send him back."

He looked tired as he rubbed his eyes. "But that's what we've got to do," he said.

And I knew he was right.

Early the next morning we got Duke ready to go. I had cleaned up the cage he came in, and we now put him back in that. He looked pretty droopy once he was inside. I put in some fresh straw and a bowl of water, but he just stood there, about half humped up and looking sort of cold.

That's how he looked when we put him on the train. I stood on the platform as the train pulled out of the station, and watched until it was out of sight.

I wished then that we had sent Duke back the minute he arrived, instead of keeping him for two weeks. Maybe then I wouldn't have felt so responsible for him.

Dad didn't look too happy about it either. I knew he was disappointed about Duke. Also, it had cost him $5.00 freight charges to send

Duke back, and I guessed he might be thinking about that too. Five dollars was about as much as Dad made in a whole day's work.

When I got home, there was a letter from Imogene. It was the second one I had gotten since our talk at Toby's. I went out to the garage to read it.

I sat down on the concrete floor. The concrete was cold and smelled a little like oil. Queenie came over and nosed at my hand as I opened the envelope.

It hadn't been a very good day, but Imogene's letter helped some. She reminded me that she was coming to Billie Jean's for three days the next week for the basketball tournament. She said she was sorry we hadn't got to sit together at the movie. Then, in a P.S., she asked me how Duke was doing. She said she thought he had a nice name.

That was a good question: just how was Duke doing? It was a two-day train trip from Oklahoma to Kentucky. Would Duke be scared in the dark freight car that whole time? Of course, there was no way he could know where he was going. I wondered what would happen to him when he got back to the kennels that had sold him to us. Would they be mean to him because we had sent him back? Would he miss us? I felt sure that he would miss Queenie and that she would miss him.

On the cold concrete Queenie felt warm and comfortable against my leg, her chin resting on my ankle. I sat there looking at the stretching-boards leaning up against the wall across the floor from us. They had been empty all winter.

For a moment I could see the civet cats with dirt in their nostrils and their eyes looking as if they had been closed carelessly. It made me feel funny.

But I couldn't stop thinking of Duke, going back to Kentucky, cold and lonely and humped up inside the cage. Right then I decided that I was going to buy him back myself. Queenie and I would just have to get enough hides together to pay for him somehow, I thought. And we would have to do that by ourselves.

It didn't seem like an easy job.

I stroked Queenie's neck and ears. She rippled her skin with pleasure. I noticed she had quite a bit of gray in her muzzle.

I put Imogene's letter in my shirt pocket and stood up. I fingered my Barlow and wondered whether she really liked Duke's name.

On Saturday morning I got started on my plan to buy back Duke: I went hunting for possums. I took Queenie with me, although in the daytime like this it was more for company than for help in hunting. I also took my rifle, though I didn't take any shells for it. It was an old bolt-action single-shot .22, which I had gotten as a present the year before.

We walked to the edge of town and followed a small creek back into the woods. I knew this area well, for I had hunted here several times with Dad. It was mostly flat, with some low hills. There wasn't much water in the creek at this time of year.

Queenie started right in hunting and it was interesting to watch her. At night you don't get to see your dog very often while it's hunting. But I could watch her work now, crossing back and forth in front of me with her nose almost touching the ground, going a little farther to each side every time, trying to find a trail. I could hear her sniffing, even above the rustling she made in the dried leaves. Of course, all the trails were cold now, so the chances of her finding anything were slim.

I had never been daytime possum-hunting by myself before, but I knew how well enough. The thing to do is keep checking hollow trees and stumps, hoping to find one that a possum is using for a den or at least as a place to sleep during the day.

Finally, along about the middle of the afternoon, I found one. I suppose I had already checked a hundred holes without any luck. At many of the ones down close to the ground there had been Queenie, snorting and plunging at the hole so that I could hardly get the prodding stick into it. They were all empty, even though Queenie seemed to smell traces of possum in two or three of them.

She could smell possum here too, but this hole was in the side of the tree, up about three feet off the ground. About all she could do was bounce around barking and whining. Now and again she would rear up on the tree and try to stick her nose in the hole, and I would have to push her away.

I was sure there was a possum in there even before I felt it—from the way Queenie was acting. Of course, the hole was so dark that I couldn't see anything past a foot or so inside it. I was feeling carefully down in the hole with a long stick, the way you have to do. Then I felt it. It was soft and gave some when I touched it with the point of the stick, but it was firm too. I knew it was a possum. It didn't come charging out of the hole or growl or anything. It just stayed there, the way a possum will, hoping I would go away, I guess. It was obviously at the bottom of the hole and couldn't move away from the stick.

I took my pocket knife and cut a branch about as big around as my thumb from the limb just above me. It had a fork near the end of it, and that's what I needed. I cut off the twigs along the branch and then the tips of the branches of the fork, so that they were only about two inches long. Now I had a stick for twisting the possum out of the hole.

I poked the twisting stick into the hole until I felt it touch the possum. Then I pushed on it some and started turning it. I felt the possum move a little as the fork in the stick bothered him. I kept pushing it against him and turning it slow, until I finally could tell that the fork was beginning to twist up in his fur. That's what I wanted. I had seen Dad and my brother do this enough times to know how. I gave the stick a couple more turns and then pulled on it good and hard. I could feel the possum really starting to struggle around down there. The stick was all twisted up tight in his fur and I was pulling on it, so he was just going to have to come out. His paws were grabbing at the sides of the hole, scratching on the wood as he came up.

Pretty soon I could see his tail just a foot or so inside the hole, all gray and smooth and sort of scaly looking. I reached in and grabbed it and gave a jerk. I knew he couldn't turn around and bite while I was pulling and he was trying to hang on to the side of the tree. Queenie was so excited now that she was scrabbling at the tree, trying to climb it.

I got both hands onto the tail, and then gave a big heave. Out the possum came. He was pretty upset and was hissing and spitting, with his mouth open and his teeth showing. Queenie jumped at him, as I swung him around and hit his head against the tree. It didn't hurt him much, but it made him do what I wanted. He went limp and pretended to be dead. I had to give Queenie a sharp slap on the muzzle to keep her off him.

I stopped to catch my breath a minute. The possum lay there like it was dead. Queenie sat looking at us sort of sad like, whining a little and moving her tail back and forth in the dead leaves.

It was a big possum and would be heavy to carry home. So I knew I had to kill it before starting back. Dad had always done the killing before, but I had watched him.

I put the possum on his stomach and laid the barrel of my rifle across his neck just behind his head. Then I put my feet on the barrel, one on each side of his head, and took his tail in my hands.

He was still pretending to be dead. I tightened my grip and started to pull up and back on the possum's tail, just as hard as I could. I could feel his neck pulling and stretching, and he was beginning to twist and squirm, trying to get loose.

He was desperate now, but the rifle barrel had him pinned tight to the ground. My face felt hot and tingling, I was pulling so hard.

Then I felt the snap. I let go of his tail and stepped away. I knew his neck was broken, but he turned and twisted on the ground like a snake, not making a sound except for the rustling of the leaves.

I suddenly felt cold and weak. I leaned against the tree. I could smell the possum, strong and heavy like.

Then I vomited.

I sat on the ground beside Queenie and leaned back against an old stump and rested for a few minutes. The possum was still now. I tried to think about how much a hide as big as this one might bring and about how I needed the money to get Duke back. But I couldn't keep my mind on it. What I kept thinking of was the possum itself.

Pretty soon I got up and picked up the possum and started back toward town, carrying it by the tail. Queenie followed along behind me, still sulking because of the slap I'd given her.

On the way home we passed by Mr. Brandts' house, and he came over to the fence to talk. I never could understand Mr. Brandts very well, because he spoke with a real thick German accent. He was always friendly though, and liked to talk. He didn't have any children. Just cats. I never did see his wife much before she died, for she always seemed to be inside the house.

Once Mr. Brandts helped put a new roof on our house, although he wasn't really a carpenter. He was the janitor at our school. But this was in the summertime, and I guess he needed the work. I noticed that he hit his thumbs a lot when he was hammering nails, but he never did seem to get mad and cuss about it the way the others did. His fingernails were black and blue all summer.

The thing I always noticed most about him though was his arms. He almost always wore short-sleeved shirts, and he had all these big lumps under the skin on his arms. Some of them were almost as big as golf balls. He had real muscular arms, and then on top of the muscles, here and there, were these round lumps. They always reminded me of the lumps

I had seen under a cow's hide in the late summer, which were caused by grubs growing under the skin. The grubs grew from eggs laid by a certain kind of fly, and the farmers had to spray their cows to try to protect them, because the grubs made holes in the hides, which made them worth less money when they were sold.

I once tried to squeeze one of those lumps out of a cow, but it just crushed inside, and some kind of bloody fluid came out of the little hole in the skin.

When I looked at the lumps on Mr. Brandts' arms, I would wonder if they were grubs and whether you could squeeze them out. I asked him about them once, and he told me they were fatty deposits under the skin, and didn't cause any trouble.

Now he reached over the fence and patted Queenie and asked me what I had been doing.

I laid the possum down in the grass beside the fence. My arm and shoulder ached from the weight of it.

"I've been hunting," I said.

He looked at the possum for a while and didn't say anything.

"I'm going to cure the hide and then sell it," I said.

Mr. Brandts still didn't say anything, just kept looking at the possum. He had his arms resting on top of the fence. It was a pretty cool day, even though the sun was shining, and it was getting late in the afternoon. But he had on a short-sleeved shirt. I could see the lumps on his arms.

He just shook his head then and said in his funny way that things seemed a lot smaller when they were dead. Then he went inside his house.

I went home and skinned the possum before supper. I felt peculiar as I did it. I think I still felt weak from vomiting, and the smell of the possum kept bringing the feeling back. Also, as I was peeling the skin away from the possum, I kept seeing those fatty lumps under Mr. Brandts' skin.

When I finished and got the skin stretched nice and tight on the board, I could see that it was a good one. There were no holes in it, and the fur was good and thick. It would probably bring $1.25 easy. But I couldn't seem to take any comfort in the thought.

·8

On Thursday night I went to the basketball tournament at the high school gym. They let students in for a dime. Our highschool team was usually one of the favorites in the tournament, so there was always a big turnout for the games. And since Billie Jean's brother was on the team, her family was always there.

I went early, for I was feeling a little depressed. I had been hunting twice since I had caught the possum, but although Queenie seemed to hunt real well each time, we didn't get anything. She just couldn't seem to tree what she was after. On the second night, I had to call her off the trail and go home even though she seemed to be on a good hot trail. It was too late and we simply had to quit. I about half suspected that she was on the trail of a coon that time and that he was just too tricky for her.

When I got to the gym, Imogene and Billie Jean were already there. I saw them sitting over by Billie Jean's uncle, Cecil Clelland. They waved and I went over to where they were.

Cecil Clelland never seemed to miss a game, day or night. You could always count on him and his wife being there, eating hamburgers and drinking cokes just like they had lots of money.

They didn't seem to notice as I came over.

Imogene had on a pink sweater that was sort of furry. She had a ribbon in her hair that was the same color, though it was smooth-looking. Her hair seemed almost black, and it looked as if all the lights in the gym were shining in it. She smiled and slid over to make room for me to sit down. I wanted to say how nice I thought she looked, but when she smiled at me, my throat suddenly felt all tight and dry. So I just sat down.

Cecil Clelland looked over at me suddenly and grinned. "Hey, Jess," he said. "Have you heard anything from your dog back in Kentucky?" But before I could say anything, he said, "No, I guess even a Black-and-Tan can't bark quite that loud." He laughed quite a bit over that.

I felt angry and embarrassed. I was glad Imogene didn't laugh.

In a minute or so Imogene asked if I would like to go outside for a while, before the game started, and I said yes.

We went outside and walked along the street next to the gym. For a few minutes we didn't talk any, just sort of loafed along, side by side. It was a dark night, and most of the time I could hardly see Imogene, even though she was so close we bumped against each other from time to time. It was like she was a slightly darker place there beside me in the dark. Except for her face. Her hair was just the color of the night, so her face seemed to float along beside me like the moon.

I stopped and sat down on a low concrete wall at the side of the schoolyard. Imogene sat down beside me. I wondered what I ought to say to her.

Finally, I asked her if she remembered the picnic we had all gone on the year before.

She said yes, she remembered.

I wanted to talk about it, to try to explain, but I didn't know how.

"I thought you were so pretty that day," I said. "And you looked, you know, so mature. Well, I wanted you to like me a lot and to think that I was mature too. And anyway, I think that the swimming was a mistake."

She kept putting one of her gloves on and then taking it off.

"That was over a year and a half ago," she said. "And besides, I like you a lot now." She stopped a moment and then said, "I also think you're a very mature person, Jess."

Then she got up, and we started walking again.

Pretty soon she asked me about Duke, and I told her what I was doing, how I was planning to buy him back and all. But I didn't mention the mixed-up feelings I'd been having.

She was silent for a while. Then she said that seemed like an awful lot of money for me to have to get and that it would take a lot of hides.

Mr. Brandts lived only about a block and a half from the gym, and we were passing by his house as Imogene said this. I could hear one of his cats crying to be let in.

It made me feel sort of good for Imogene to think that was a lot of money for me to raise. It made me feel as though I almost had the money already. And I felt like going right out and catching a coon.

I said, yes, I'd thought about how much money it was.

The cat cried again, and it sounded sort of sad. I looked up and saw a light in Mr. Brandts' house, and I thought about the possum.

Then suddenly I was telling her about killing the possum and about getting sick and about skinning it and everything. I could almost smell the heavy scent of the possum, and it made me choke a little as I talked. Imogene looked at me as we turned the corner and started back toward the gym, and then she reached over and took hold of my hand very tight as she said, "I'm glad you told me about that, Jess. I really am."

I was glad too.

We didn't talk any the rest of the way back, but we did touch hands just before we went inside. And going up the steps we were so close I could smell Imogene's hair.

Inside the gym the air was hot and seemed heavy. The game had started while we were outside, and the crowd was already making a lot of noise. I tried to remember how Imogene's hair had smelled outside, but the air was too hot. I kept thinking first of the possum and then of the civet cats. And for some reason I felt, just for a moment, as if I had dirt in my nostrils.

·9

I didn't go to the basketball tournament Friday night, even though our team was in the semi-finals. I wanted to go, and to see Imogene. But I knew I had to get busy if I was ever going to get enough money to buy back Duke. So Queenie and I went hunting.

This time Queenie treed her possum. I guess she struck a really hot trail right at the start, so there wasn't much chance of her losing it. She was really pleased with herself as I stood under the tree and pointed my flashlight up into the dark. I could make out the possum perched on a limb right next to the trunk, about halfway up the tree. It had the side of its head turned toward me, so that I could see only one eye, looking green in the light beam. I guess Queenie could see it too because she just about went crazy. I thought I'd never get her calmed down, even after I got the possum out of the tree. She acted like it was the first time she had ever treed a possum. It got me pretty excited too.

All the way home I could tell how happy she was by the way she trotted along just a little ways in front of me, but not checking the ditches along the road or anything. I wished Duke had been in on it. I felt sure he would have learned something from it.

I went to bed thinking about that.

After breakfast next morning, I went out to the garage to skin the possum. But I had a hard time getting started.

The sun was shining on the side of the garage as I laid the possum down on the ground beside it. The sun felt warm on my back, and I shivered a little at the feel of it. For a while I just stood there looking at the possum. It looked all gray and wintry in the sun. And as Mr. Brandts had said, it did look smaller dead.

Queenie came over and sat down on her haunches to watch. Her broad back looked like coal in the sunlight, about half black and half silver, though it was really solid black. She didn't seem much interested in the possum anymore.

I sat down on the grass and whetted my knife on the side of my shoe, trying not to think about the possum either. I thought instead about how smooth and shiny the knife blade made the leather I whetted it on. From time to time I checked the blade for sharpness by trying to shave the hair on my arm. I always spit on the hair first to make it wet.

Dad came out to the garage once and asked me what was wrong, and I said, "Nothing."

He already knew about my plan to buy back Duke. I had told him the night before. Now he stood around for a few minutes just watching me do nothing. Then after a while he said, "Would you like me to help you with the possum?"

I shook my head no but didn't say anything, and Dad went back in the house.

So when I finally finished, Dad asked me if I wanted to go downtown with him. He said he thought I would like to get away for a while. And I said yes.

We were both quiet in the car at first. Dad looked over at me a couple of times, like he was trying to figure out what I was thinking. But he didn't say anything and just kept driving.

As we were passing the schoolhouse, a cat ran across the street in front of us. Dad stepped on the brakes, though I don't think it was really that close. I watched the cat run up on the porch of a house as we went on past.

"A cat's an interesting animal," Dad said, jerking his head toward the side of the road where the cat had been. "Even though it's tame and gets plenty to eat at home, it still goes hunting, hoping to catch something and kill it. It's just something it needs to do, I guess. I even had a cat once that brought home a dead field mouse one morning and then stood at the door meowing until I came and opened it. Then it put the mouse down at my feet and purred and rubbed up against my legs just as if it was real pleased about it."

He seemed to stop and think about that for a moment before he said, "You know, I really think it meant that mouse as a present for me."

We stopped in front of the Masonic Hall.

"Of course, I didn't really have much use for it," he said, and looked over at me and smiled a little.

I smiled back but couldn't think of anything to say just then.

Dad parked the car and didn't say anything for a minute or two. Then he said, "I learned to hunt when I was just a little boy, Jess. And I've hunted ever since. I guess it's almost as natural to me now as it is to a cat." He set the handbrake and looked out the window. "But sometimes a person can't help wondering about it when he looks at the dead animal next morning."

He started to get out of the car, and then turned back and said, "But then I don't suppose a cat ever does that, does he?"

We got out of the car and walked over to Garrett's Grocery Store. We always bought groceries on credit there, and Dad paid Mr. Garrett every month.

I stood around by the magazine rack at the front of the store while Dad and Mr. Garrett went over to the cash register and looked at the book. There was a *Rod and Gun* magazine in the rack with a picture of a man and a dog hunting. The man had on an expensive-looking jacket with lots of pockets and shells in it, and he had a gun sort of cradled in the crook of his arm. I didn't think he looked like much of a hunter. I thought the dog looked a bit like Duke, but it was hard to tell.

I heard Dad say, kind of loud, "Camay, the soap of beautiful women." And I looked up from the *Rod and Gun.*

The only other person in the store was a woman standing over by a counter that had a sign above it reading "Beauty Aids," though Mr. Garrett didn't really have a lot of stuff on it. Just shampoo and soap and things like that. The woman looked real poor and didn't have on any makeup, not even lipstick. Her dress seemed too big for her, she was so skinny. She looked pretty young, but her hair looked old, and it was all wispy and sort of gathered into a knot.

She had a bar of soap in her hand and was looking over at Dad and Mr. Garrett.

"Yes, sir," Dad said, "Camay will give you a

cleaner skin and a finer complexion, just like the movie stars."

I almost expected him to say "unquote." He winked at Mr. Garrett, but the woman didn't see him.

She was looking at the bar of soap again, and she had a funny look on her face, like she might either smile or cry any minute.

"Do you really think so?" she said.

Dad looked over at Mr. Garrett and then down at his hands. "Sure," he said, not very loud.

I was beginning to feel uncomfortable. Dad took out his billfold and started counting out the money for our bill. He took a long time at it. He didn't look up when the woman paid for the soap.

Mr. Garrett kept sorting money in the cash register all the time she was leaving the store.

When we got home, we all sat down around the dining table and divided up the big sack of candy Mr. Garrett always gave Dad for paying his bill. We all took equal shares to eat later. It was a kind of game.

We usually had a good time when we did this and would laugh and talk a lot. But we were quiet today. Mom wanted to know what was wrong, and Dad told her about the woman and the soap. He told it like a joke, but he didn't laugh any.

Neither did Mother.

I took my share of the candy and went to my room. I lay down on the bed and looked out the window. I could see the boards with the possum skins drying in the sun. I tried to think about how Dad and my brother had smoothed the boards by scraping them with a piece of broken glass until they were almost as smooth as glass themselves. But I kept thinking of a lot of things all at the same time—the possums, and Duke, and Imogene, and the woman at Garrett's Grocery Store. I wondered if that woman had ever had $50.00 all at one time.

·10

The next morning I went squirrel hunting with Maurice Wapanucka and Joe Hooker. Of course, this wouldn't help get money for Duke. But I wanted to be with someone and to relax.

We didn't take Queenie because we planned just to sight hunt, and anyway half the fun of squirrel hunting in the daytime is being in the quiet woods, and talking some when you feel like it. So we didn't need the sound of Queenie barking all over the place while we were hunting. Besides, she would just scare the squirrels so that they would all go in their holes or nests, and we wouldn't be able to see any. I had to tie her up when we left.

We took our rifles, but we carried the shells in our pockets. We would load them when we got to the woods. Joe didn't have a rifle of his own, so he took his dad's. It was a .22 bolt-action, with the magazine under the barrel.

I had been hunting lots of times with Maurice, but we had never been out with Joe before. I didn't really know him very well, mostly just from seeing him at school. Maurice was an Indian, and he was pretty tall, though kind of skinny. His waist wasn't much bigger than a wasp's. Joe was the same age as we were, but bigger. He was about as tall as Maurice, although a lot heavier, about the size of Maurice's dad. I had heard he was a fine football player.

It was a good day for squirrel hunting. The sun was bright and warm, the way you need it. The squirrels like to come out onto the limbs and stretch out in the sun, just like somebody sunbathing. What you have to look for is some sign of the squirrel lying there—like the bush of his tail hanging off to one side of the limb or maybe some movement of the tail to give him away. Sometimes you can spot a fox squirrel just by color, seeing that little patch of reddish-brown against the gray limbs, but you have to be pretty sharp-eyed to do that, and lucky.

We all sat down and loaded our rifles beside the lake at the power plant. Then we went into the woods that ran all along one side of it and then off the other direction from town. It was a pretty good place for squirrel hunting, though it was not too good for possum hunting. I had been there a few times with Maurice and also with Dad.

It was nice in the woods. Mostly all you

could hear was the sound of the dead leaves rustling and crackling as you walked. It felt good to walk in and out of the shadows of the trees. Of course, there weren't any leaves on the trees, so the shadows were pretty thin, just enough to make you feel the sun better every time you stepped into it. Sometimes when Maurice and I would come hunting here, we would walk along for ten or fifteen minutes at a time without saying anything. I wanted to just sort of enjoy the quiet now. But Joe simply wouldn't shut up.

Ever since we had left home he had been talking steadily. And after we loaded the guns he seemed to get even worse. He kept doing things like shouting, "All right, squirrels, I'm ready for you. Just give me a little target, an eye or something." And then he would jerk his rifle up to his shoulder and point it at some tree and pretend he was shooting. It was pretty silly, and both Maurice and I told him to stop two or three times. But that only seemed to make him do it more.

I could see that Maurice was getting upset. He never did talk a lot, but I could tell by the way he was holding his mouth he didn't like what was going on. I had been to Maurice's house quite a few times, and I knew that he didn't like silliness. Even the times when I had played Indian dice with him and his family, there hadn't been any very loud laughing or shouting or anything. One of them would take the shallow wooden bowl and throw the little hand-carved wooden animals in some kind of pattern on the floor. If they got a good throw or won the game or something, they would laugh and sort of kid the other players, but they never were real loud about it.

And, of course, Joe was being foolish and careless about the rifle.

So along about noon Maurice said he thought we ought to go back home. Naturally, we hadn't seen even one squirrel, what with Joe whooping and shouting around.

Joe argued quite a bit when Maurice said this. But we both said we were leaving, so when we started back toward the lake he came along too. He kept saying that we hadn't had any fun and that he didn't want to go back home without having any fun.

We came out of the woods farther down the lake from where we went in, right where an old cemetery was at the edge of the woods. We started across the cemetery to get to the road back to town.

I was the last one to crawl through the barbed wire fence bordering the cemetery. I had just got through and picked up my rifle when Joe said, "All right. Let's each get behind a tombstone and have a shoot-out, each one against the other two."

I didn't think it was very funny, and I guess Maurice didn't either, because we both started off across the cemetery without even saying anything.

Suddenly Joe ran around in front of us and jumped behind a big pink granite tombstone. He pointed his rifle at us.

"Okay, you'd better take cover, because I'm going to start shooting any minute."

He was smiling all the time he said this, but he had a funny look in his eye I thought.

"Come on, Joe," Maurice said. "That's enough of that. It's dangerous pointing that loaded rifle at us."

I thought so too, and I said I thought we ought to unload our rifles now, since we had finished hunting.

Joe just kept pointing the rifle at us, and then he flipped the bolt and shoved a shell into the firing chamber.

"Better pick a tombstone," he said. He was still smiling, but not quite as wide as before.

Maurice and I looked at each other, and I could see that he was as worried as I was. I had learned to shoot when I was eight, and I knew never to play with a rifle. I simply couldn't believe that someone would actually point a loaded gun at someone else while playing a kid's game of pretend war or something.

Both Marurice and I told him that we didn't like it and that we wanted him to quit. We started walking on again, planning to walk right past him.

Then Joe actually sighted down the rifle barrel at Maurice.

"Right in the eye, just like a squirrel—unless you get a tombstone," he said.

We both stopped and stood there in the graveyard with the tombstones all around us. I could hear an airplane somewhere far off, but there was no other sound. Maurice shifted his feet uneasy like.

I started to feel scared. I thought Joe had to be joking about shooting Maurice, and the whole thing was so crazy that I about half felt like it wasn't happening.

But it was.

"We came to do some shootin' so let's do some shootin'," Joe said. I thought he really looked strange now. "We won't really shoot each other. Just the tombstones—if you pick a tombstone."

Of course, that was crazy too, I thought. Nobody could want to do that kind of thing. I looked at Joe, trying to figure out what he was thinking. It was still January, and even in the sun there was a touch of cool in the air. But I felt hot and sweaty. I bent over and laid my .22 on the ground. My mouth felt all dry.

I told Joe that if he didn't stop, someone might accidentally get shot and that we would all be in trouble.

Maurice laid his rifle down too.

"You're both scared," Joe said. "Aintcha? You're afraid to have a shoot-out."

I told him yes, I was afraid. Which was true. Maurice said he was too.

For a few minutes we all just stayed there like that—Maurice and me standing sort of side by side and Joe kneeling behind the tombstone. Then all of a sudden Joe got up and lowered the rifle. "Okay," he said. "Forget it." And he started unloading the magazine of the .22.

I felt strange as I took the shell out of my gun. I felt almost like this was happening to someone else and that I was just looking on. It made me sort of dizzy, and I sat down on the ground for a couple of minutes. Pretty soon Maurice said we'd better go.

On the way home Joe acted just like nothing had happened. He laughed and talked and waved his hands around as he walked, and a little while before we got back to Maurice's house, he said of course he had just been joking back there in the cemetery. He said he had just been checking to see what we would do. Then he smiled real big and started talking about football.

Maurice and I didn't say anything then, and when we got to the Wapanuckas' house, we separated and I went on home.

I thought about what had happened there in

the cemetery. And I thought it must have been a joke like Joe said.

But the rifle felt awfully heavy in my hand the rest of the way. I was even glad we hadn't seen any squirrels.

When I got home, I put the .22 up and went out to check the possum hides. I didn't say anything to Mother or Dad about the squirrel hunt.

After supper I wrote Imogene a letter. I had been thinking quite a bit about Duke and how the hunting was going, which wasn't too well. I had to admit that the $50.00 was looking like a bigger amount all the time. And I told Imogene so in the letter.

Not that I had given up. I hadn't. But it was getting harder. And the hunting wasn't as much fun as before. I wished that I could see Imogene, so I asked her when she thought she might be visiting Billie Jean again. I was hoping it might be soon because I felt better when I talked to Imogene.

When I went to bed, I couldn't go to sleep for a long time, even though I was tired. I kept thinking about what had happened with Maurice Wapanucka and Joe Hooker, and the whole thing bothered me. I kept telling myself that nothing bad had happened and that Joe had only been playing a stupid kind of joke. But I couldn't keep my eyes off my .22 standing over in the corner of the room. Finally I got up and put it in my closet so that I couldn't see it.

After that I kept thinking how beautiful Imogene had been the last time I saw her, with the moon shining on her hair and making it look like it was glowing from inside itself. I finally went to sleep, half dreaming that Imogene's black hair was wrapping around me warm and soft like a thick fur.

The next morning I mailed the letter first thing after breakfast. It wasn't until that afternoon, after I got home from school, that I got the letter from my brother. My brother was nineteen and had been in the army almost a year. He had gone away to look for work after he finished high school, but there weren't many jobs around. Finally he joined the army, mostly out of desperation, I guess.

He told me he had heard about Duke from Dad and that he was writing to tell me he was sorry. He enclosed a check for $20.00, which he said he hoped would help me get enough money to buy Duke back.

This made me feel better than I had for days. I was grateful to my brother. I knew he had other things to do with his money. He didn't get paid very much in the army, and I knew that he sometimes sent Mother and Dad some money to help out.

I figured he was probably remembering Ladd. The fact is, I had thought about Ladd myself when we sent Duke back to Kentucky. I even suspected that Dad was remembering him and being a bit sad about it.

Ladd was one of Queenie's pups, the only one we had ever kept. We had always sold all the others because they brought a pretty good price when they were weaned—especially the males. But there was something about Ladd even when he was just a tiny puppy that made Dad and my brother want to keep him. I think it was mostly his feet and his ears. They were bigger than any of the other pups had, and Dad said they were the biggest he had ever seen on a pup that age. So that seemed a good sign he would grow up to be a really good hunting dog. And he was a thoroughbred Black-and-Tan.

Ladd really belonged to my brother, who was about my age then. But Dad was just as proud of him as he could be. As Ladd got bigger and the rest of him started growing up to his ears and feet, Dad just couldn't stop bragging about him and what a great hunting dog he was going to be.

I think I got to go with them the first time they took him out on a daytime hunt, although I was only about eight or nine years old. Ladd must have been four months old then, and he was still more feet and ears and tummy than anything else. But he loved that hunt. He tried to follow Queenie when he heard her bay, but he never could get out of our sight. In fact, he spent most of the time behind us, trying to catch up. He was still awfully clumsy, so that when he tried to run he fell down every few feet. Whenever there was a fallen tree or log across our trail, someone had to help him over it. He never did seem to think of going around it.

When Ladd was about nine months old, he really started to look and act like a hunting hound. By that time he was taller than Queenie by a little, and although he didn't weigh as much, he had a bigger frame and bones.

I don't think Dad will ever forget the first time Ladd bayed on the trail. It was a real coon hunt, when Queenie was still one of the finest dogs in the area. Of course, if there was any real hunting instinct in Ladd, Queenie would bring it out. She could teach him plenty, too.

Dad and my brother and I were just sort of standing around in the dark, stamping our feet now and then to keep them from getting too cold and waiting for Queenie to strike a trail. A screech owl yelled nearby, and I moved over a little closer to Dad. There wasn't any moon, so it was real dark.

Then Queenie sounded a trail, and we

started to walk slowly in her direction. You could already tell that she was moving away from us pretty fast. It sounded like a hot one.

I guess we had all sort of forgotten about Ladd. We were used to him being there with Queenie, trying to learn to hunt but not really doing anything. Now all of a sudden he bayed on the trail, just behind Queenie. It was so loud and sudden that we all jumped a bit. They must have been half a mile away by that time, but Ladd's voice was so loud that it made your ears ring. It started out kind of low, and then rose up to a high note right at the end, almost as though his voice was changing. Both Dad and my brother grinned and gave out big whoops and shouts. And having Ladd's voice added to everything was sort of like having electricity in the air.

They treed a coon about half an hour later, and Ladd was right in on the baying that told us they had it up a tree. There's no mistaking the sound a dog makes when he has the animal cornered like that, once you've heard it. And Ladd was sure doing his part of the calling. Dad said he figured Ladd learned more about coon hunting from that one experience than lots of dogs do in their entire lives. I think that he was probably right.

It was about six months later, in the summer, when it happened. Almost no one in our town kept dogs penned up or anything. So Ladd had run free most of the time all his life. He had always stuck pretty close to home with Queenie. I don't suppose he had ever been completely out of range of our voice, so that even if he did wander away he always came running when we called—especially to my brother's voice.

One day in July he didn't come home when my brother called him to give him his supper. He still wasn't home when it got dark. We all took turns calling him, and my brother rode all around that part of town on his bicycle, calling his name and whistling. All the calling and whistling must have made Queenie pretty nervous because she kept whining kind of softly and going over and sitting down by the feet of one after the other of us. But Ladd still didn't come.

Just before I went to bed I stood out in the yard with my brother, taking turns calling. Every now and then we would hear some other dog somewhere in town bark, as if in answer. And Queenie came over and whined some more.

There was already dew on the grass, and it made my shoes almost soaking wet. But the night was warm and I didn't mind. There were so many fireflies you could hardly see the stars. I thought my brother looked pretty worried.

When we went back inside, Dad said Ladd would probably be home in the morning, but he didn't sound as if he believed it.

Ladd wasn't home the next morning. And we were all pretty quiet at breakfast. Dad looked like he hadn't slept much.

"I just don't understand why he hasn't come home yet," my brother said. "He just has to be hurt or killed."

"Maybe not," Mother said. "He's a fine-looking dog. Maybe someone has him shut up so that he can't come home. We'll just have to try to find him."

All that morning my brother combed the town, looking for him. At lunch he was very discouraged. He had called to Ladd and asked people, but no one had seen or heard anything that might help.

After lunch my brother decided to look for him outside of town and to check the farm roads nearby.

I said I would keep looking in town.

I was just coming out of the house about 4 o'clock when my brother came through the gate with Ladd in his arms. Ladd's head was hanging down a little bit, over the bend in my brother's arm, and I could see the blood on it. I guess I must have screamed or something because Mother came running out of the house just then and took Ladd in her arms.

He was so heavy she staggered a little at

first. Then she took him up on the porch and laid him down. She took off her apron and put it under his head. I could see that he was alive, but his eyes were shut and he looked real bad.

My brother still hadn't said anything, and Mother asked him what had happened.

At first he didn't answer. He just stood there, smiling and blinking, the way he would do when he was trying to keep from crying. Then he said, "He got hit by a car," and ran into the house. I could hear the sound of crying, muffled by the bed, coming from inside.

Later he fixed up a special bed for Ladd in the garage and took him out there. He tried to give him some water, but Ladd couldn't drink it, though he must have been awful thirsty.

A farmer about a mile outside of town had helped my brother find Ladd. My brother had asked him if he had seen a young Black-and-Tan hound. He had remembered that a man had stopped at his house the day before, about noon, asking for some water for a dog that was hurt. Of course, the farmer didn't know that the dog had been hit by a car or that it was lying in a ditch off at the side of the road.

My brother had gone searching along the road then, hoping he wouldn't find him, or that it wasn't Ladd that had been hurt. But he found him in a ditch, about half a mile from the farmer's house, partly hidden by the weeds. He had been there in the sun for more than a day.

When Dad came home, he checked Ladd's head, and you could tell that he was hurt too bad to get well. One side of his head was sort of soft from where the car had hit it. Dad looked real white.

When my brother told him about the man stopping for the water, Dad got very angry. He said he was sure that was the car that had hit Ladd and why hadn't the driver at least taken Ladd over to the farmer's house? He said someone ought to be horsewhipped for that sort of thing.

The way I look at it is, at least the man had stopped and tried to get Ladd a drink. He probably couldn't help it that he had run into him with his car.

My brother stayed all night with Ladd in the garage in case he needed him. He must have been very tired, for he had carried Ladd in his arms for about three miles. Mother didn't want him to stay out there all night, but Dad said it was O.K.

Ladd didn't die until the next morning, though I think we all knew he was going to. It still hit us awfully hard when he did. Everyone of us cried, including Mother, who had always fussed about how much Ladd ate.

Dad never got over wanting to get another good hunting dog after that, but he and my brother never wanted to keep another one of Queenie's pups.

I put my brother's check for $20.00 in a drawer and went out into the yard. Queenie came over to nuzzle my hand. It was getting cold and the wind was out of the north. The sky was kind of gray and spitting out small flakes of snow. I went over and got the two boards with possum hides on them and took them into the garage. The hides were stiff and hard from the cold.

·12

During the rest of that week, Mother and Dad wouldn't let me go hunting at night. They said I needed to stay home and rest and do my school work. It was just as well. The weather was cold and wet, so I don't think Queenie could have treed even a possum, much less a coon, which I now realized is what we had to get if we were ever going to get the money for Duke.

I was pretty restless for the next few days.

I just couldn't get things to straighten out in my mind. I didn't seem to want to have money so much any more. But, of course, I needed it to buy back Duke. And then there was Imogene. And Mr. Brandts. And me. The trouble was, I just didn't know what to think about me.

Late Wednesday afternoon I was sitting around trying to think about everything, and Dad came into the house through the back door and shouted,

"Hey, you two. Come in here."

When Mother and I went into the kitchen, there he was, in the middle of the room, turning around and around and holding out the bottom of a new black mackinaw jacket with each hand. And he was grinning like a possum.

"I thought I might as well get something that would match the patching material," he said. He turned slowly around once more.

"With the money I saved on Duke, I thought we could afford it," he said. "Besides, it'll save you having to do so much patching." He put his arm around Mother's shoulders.

"Unquote," Mother said. She was smiling when she said it.

"Who knows? I might even have enough time now to go to the movies next time Toby comes to town," she said, "that is, if Jess won't mind lending me some of the potatoes he didn't trade."

We all laughed more than we had in quite a while.

On Monday I got a letter from Imogene, and I could hardly wait to open it. I had been thinking a lot about her all week, and I wanted to talk to her.

I took the letter to my room and opened it.

Dear Jess,

It's cold and rainy here today, and I am just sitting here in my room, wishing I could see you and talk to you. It's too wet even to go horseback riding, and I don't really want to anyway. I have been remembering the talk we had last time we were together and how glad I am about it all. I hope you are too.

Now here's the good news. Saturday I'm coming to visit Billie Jean, and I will stay Saturday night and all of Sunday. We will plan to do something together, probably on Saturday night, O.K.?

Can't wait to see you.

Love,
Imogene

P.S.
I think it's a very fine thing you've been doing, trying to earn enough money to buy back Duke. And I'm very proud of you for it. I think you've been very brave and very mature. But I also know how you feel about the possum and everything. So I keep wondering if maybe Duke doesn't cost too much.

The letter was written on a sort of violet-colored paper, and even the envelope was made of the same paper. It smelled just a little bit like perfume.

I put the letter back in the envelope and put it in the drawer with the check.

·13

The next day I asked Maurice Wapanucka if he would go hunting with me that night and he said yes. I knew I had to go since I was still so far from the $50.00 I needed for Duke, but this time my heart wasn't in it and I felt like having some company. So I was glad Maurice was going with me. He was a good hunter, and he was also the kind of person who will let you be alone with your thoughts when you want to be. And I didn't feel like talking very much.

We started from my house about half an hour after supper. Queenie frisked off ahead of us in the growing darkness, every now and then trotting back into view on the road in front of us, making sure we were still coming, I guess. Then she would be off into the dark again. I knew that's what she would be doing all the way to the woods.

For the first couple of blocks we walked along without talking, watching Queenie move in and out of sight. I don't know what Maurice was thinking about, but I was thinking about

Duke and Imogene and about what I was doing.

I almost didn't notice the house we were passing, I was so deep in my thoughts. But some noise or something caught my attention and I saw where we were.

When I was about six or seven, the people who lived in that house had kept chickens in their back yard. But as often as not someone would leave the gate open and their red rooster would wander in and out of the yard pretty much the way Queenie was going in and out of the darkness now. So I never knew, when I would start to pass that house on my way to or from school, whether the rooster was going to be out or in. If he was outside (or even if he was inside the yard but near the open gate) he would come dashing toward me with his beak jutting out in front and his red neck-feathers all fluffed out, just as if he was going to bury himself right up to his shoulders in my leg. I was scared helpless, and he knew it.

Every day I tried to figure some way to get past without him seeing me. Sometimes I would sneak along the side of that yard, as carefully and as quietly as I could, until I got almost to the gate. Then I would wait. When the rooster was looking the other way, I would sneak on past the gate, hoping to get by before he saw me. Or sometimes I would wait until he was turned away and then make a sudden dash for it.

But it didn't seem to matter. If the gate was open, there he would come, right behind me. I would run to save my life.

It never occurred to me to stop and stand my ground. At times when I would tell Mother about it she would say, "It's only a rooster, for goodness' sake. A big boy like you? Just stop and give it a swift kick next time it chases you and that'll be the end of that." But I knew better. I knew that if I ever stopped when that rooster was after me, I was done for.

Sometimes he would chase me for almost half a block before he would quit, and I would be so weak that I could barely stand up.

So some days, coming home from school, I would go three or four blocks out of my way rather than face him. At times like that I could just picture him strutting around the yard, lifting his foot high off the ground with each step he took, with one eye on the open gate, watching for me.

I told Maurice about it as we walked along, and he laughed so hard I finally told him to stop or he might wake up that old rooster.

Then we both laughed some more.

By that time we were approaching the gym at school. I was surprised to see cars parked alongside it and lights showing through all the windows. I could even hear the sounds of a basketball game coming from inside. I had been fretting about Duke and hunting and things so much all day that I hadn't realized there was a game that night. I didn't even know who was playing.

Without either of us saying anything, we started a shortcut across the school ground. The front of the gym was all lighted up, but the wide steps up to the front doors were empty and the doors were shut. Everyone was inside. We could hear them clearly now, shouting at the teams and at the referees. Queenie came back around the corner of the building into the light for a look at us and then wheeled back into the dark. We followed her around the corner and along the side of the building.

It was very dark on this side, but near the back of the building one of the exit doors stood open and the light from inside reached out and down to the bottom of the steps.

As we came nearer, I could see two men just outside the glare of the light, standing to one side of the steps, facing each other. They were talking and I could tell that they were angry, but I couldn't hear what they were saying. One of the men was much bigger than the other one, broad and heavy-looking. He made the other man look small and frail.

Maurice and I were still outside the light,

about twenty feet away. So I guess the men couldn't see us. Anyway, they didn't seem to know we were there.

Just then our team must have scored or something, because everyone in the gym seemed to start yelling. At the same time, the bigger man reached out, grabbed the other man by the front of the shirt, and jerked him toward him.

I stopped where I was. I couldn't hear the sound of the men's voices above the roar of the crowd, though I could see that the bigger man was shouting something at the other one, who was jerking back and twisting about, trying to get loose.

Then the big man slapped him in the face with his free hand, and I saw the smaller man pull out of his back pocket what looked like a piece of metal pipe about a foot long. He raised it up above his head and chopped it down hard once onto the other man's head and face.

It's strange how the big man fell after he was hit. He didn't fall over backward or anything, like they do in the movies. He just stood right where he was for a moment, steadily drawing his right leg up until his knee was up against his stomach, almost like in slow motion. Then he simply dropped to the ground, falling slightly over to one side. He didn't seem to make a sound. Even the crowd inside was suddenly quiet.

The smaller man stood looking down at him for a few seconds. Then he looked up and started turning his head back and forth from side to side, as if trying to decide what to do. I guess he must have seen us then, for he suddenly stopped moving his head and stood very still, looking straight at us.

As he stood there, the light from the door shone on the side of his face, so I could see him very clearly, and I recognized him as a fellow who had been in high school with my brother and who had even come over to our house once or twice. I remembered that his name was Wade. His eyes looked very wide, and I could tell that he was scared.

He didn't say a word to us. Maybe he couldn't even see who we were there in the darkness outside of the light. He just looked at us and then, almost as if it was a signal, as the crowd started to yell again he whirled around and ran off into the night across the school yard, away from the gym, in the same direction we had been going.

It had all happened so fast. But now I looked at the man lying very still on the brown grass, half in and half out of the light, and all at once I was scared.

Maurice and I still didn't say anything. I guess maybe we were afraid to. But I knew we had to do something. I looked at Maurice and he nodded, as if I had asked him a question, even though I hadn't said anything. And maybe I had.

Anyway we walked slowly over to where the man was on the ground and looked down at him. He appeared to be hurt real bad. His face, which was only partly in the light, looked sort of gray, and there was a long cut running up alongside his nose and onto his forehead. The flesh on each side of it was puffing out like an innertube squeezing out of a cut tire. There was not much blood, just a small trickle moving back across his forehead to his hairline. I couldn't tell whether he was breathing or not.

I bent over closer to see, and then I heard a rushing noise coming around the back of the gym toward us. I straightened up and started backing away. Just as Queenie came running into the light, her tongue hanging our of her open mouth, I heard Maurice say, almost in a whisper, "Uncle Ed."

"What?" I said. "Do you know him, Maurice?"

Queenie came over and nosed at the man's ear, pushing at it as if trying to make him move. I got her by the collar and pulled her away.

"That's my uncle Ed," Maurice said, not moving his head at all, but just staring straight down at the pale, still face. "Carl Maytubby's dad."

"Come on," I said, "we've got to get help. I'll run over to Mr. Brandts' house and call the ambulance. You better go tell your folks."

We both ran off into the dark again, in separate directions, Queenie bounding off ahead of me into the night, no doubt puzzled about what we were hunting for this time and where we might be headed.

·14

As excited and troubled as I was by the evening's events, I was still pretty sleepy by the time the police got to our house. Mother and Dad had called them as soon as I got home from Mr. Brandts' and told them what had happened. Since then I had just been sitting around waiting for them to come, "so we can ask him some more questions," they'd said over the phone.

I was thinking again about all the things that had been happening to me lately. "Terrible things we do to each other," Mr. Brandts had said after I'd called the ambulance, shaking his head and rubbing his knotty arms. "As if we didn't all die soon enough anyway," though he couldn't say his *w*'s right; he made them sound more like *v*'s.

Queenie was whining and trembling as she sat on her haunches beside me, waiting for me to finish my business. Maybe she was upset by the smell of Mr. Brandts' cats.

So I didn't stay around his house any longer.

Besides, I couldn't think of any kind of reply. As usual Mr. Brandts had managed to get me thinking in a way that made me uneasy and uncertain.

Queenie and I ran most of the way home.

Mother made me a sandwich and some hot chocolate, but I didn't feel very hungry.

The main thing the policemen wanted to know was what the man who hit Maurice's uncle looked like. They'd already asked Maurice, but they wanted to hear it from me too.

"Was he tall, short, medium-sized, or what?" one of the policemen said. I told them as best I could and then went on to give them other details about him, about how young he looked, what color his hair was, and so on. But for some reason I didn't seem to want to do the simple thing and tell them I knew who he was. I didn't know why that was, but there I was doing it, and I realized that I hadn't even told Maurice.

"How bad off is Mr. Maytubby?" I asked, after I had given them a pretty good description of Wade.

One of the policemen was young, not much older than Wade or my brother. "He's got a fractured skull," he said. "The doctors say he's in pretty bad shape, critical condition. He may not make it."

I wondered why the room seemed so close then. I had to take several deep breaths to get enough air. I could clearly see in my mind the picture of Maurice's uncle lying on the ground, awkward and still, and Wade running off toward the woods where we had planned to hunt possums.

"I think his name is Wade," I said. "He used to go to school with my brother. Actually, I'm pretty sure that's who it was."

After the policemen left, Dad walked over and stood beside where I was still sitting at the kitchen table and about halfway draped his arm across my shoulders. He must have waited at least a minute before he said anything. Then finally he said, "It's peculiar, isn't it, Jess? A person starts off doing one clear, simple thing and first thing he knows he's doing something else. And then what he started off to do doesn't seem very clear or very simple either after that."

"All on account of getting that fool dog in the first place," Mother said. "That's simple enough at least."

But her heart didn't seem to be in what she said, and it didn't sound much like scolding. She stood staring into the dark outside the kitchen window, as if she could actually see the backyard in spite of the darkness, as if she could even see Queenie, sitting out there beside her kennel, listening to sounds that we could not hear. Maybe, I thought, Mother is even seeing Duke out there in the yard again.

I stood up and peered through the window, trying to discover what she might see there in the night. But all I saw was a confusion of images from my own mind.

Mother tossed her head once or twice to shake her hair free from her neck, but she kept on looking out into the night—whatever she might have been seeing there or in her mind. Her mouth looked sad and hurt, like the mouth of the woman who had bought the Camay soap.

·15

"I wonder what they were fighting about?" I said. Maurice and I were sitting on the ground, leaning back against our garage. It was beginning to get dark and rather chilly.

"I don't know," Maurice said. "I never knew Uncle Ed very well. He didn't come into town much, just stayed out there on his ranch most of the time. But when he did come to town, he usually drank a lot and sometimes got into fights."

"My dad says he knifed somebody once in a fight."

"Maybe so," Maurice said. "I was always sort of scared of him."

I nodded. "Dad says just about everybody was." I got up and walked around to the other side of Maurice, just to have something to do. "He sure was big."

Maurice had come over after supper, not long after the hospital had called to say that his uncle had died. We really hadn't talked very much—just sat around in the kitchen for a while, and then we had come outside. Being outside seemed to make it easier to talk about it.

I sat down beside Maurice again. "I wonder when they'll catch him."

Maurice put his hands in his jacket pockets. "The Sheriff came by our house just before I left and said they were pretty sure Wade was somewhere in the woods. He said they were sending for bloodhounds to help them find him, now that Uncle Ed had died."

It was fully dark now. Queenie came over and stretched out beside me. She looked almost like a shadow lying on the ground. I stroked the deep thick fur along the back of her neck. Everything was very quiet.

Then we heard it, a long ways off but clear—the throaty sound of bloodhounds baying. Sounded like three, maybe four. I thought I felt some quiver along Queenie's neck, as if she had heard them. But she didn't move.

"I think I better be going," Maurice said, getting to his feet.

Queenie and I got up too. "Yeah," I said, wanting to go inside.

We all three stood there in the dark together for a few seconds. Then Maurice turned and walked toward the gate. Queenie walked beside me to the back door. The bloodhounds were still baying, though farther away than ever.

Early the next morning, even before breakfast, a policeman came to the door and asked me and Dad to step over to the police car for a minute. It was the same young policeman of the night before last.

Another policeman was sitting in the driver's seat.

"Is that him?" he said, pointing back over the seat toward the back. The space between the front and back seats was filled all the way to the ceiling with a heavy wire mesh, making the back seat like a cage.

I looked in through the closed rear window. There sat Wade in the back seat, with handcuffs on his wrists. His clothes were dirty and torn and his hair was hanging down around his face. I could see dirt all along one side of his face, as if he had been lying on the ground on that side. He looked tired but scared.

I nodded to the policeman.

"Hello, Wade," Dad said, as he stood beside the car. "Remember me?"

Wade nodded and cleared his throat as if he wanted to speak. But he didn't say anything.

"Well, thanks a lot," the young policeman said, and got back into the car. "Sorry to have bothered you so early, but we didn't catch him until just a little while ago."

Then they drove off.

Dad and I stood alongside the street watching them disappear around a corner. We turned back toward the house.

"What do you think will happen to him?" I said.

"Hard to say," Dad said. "He did kill a man, of course, even though he probably didn't mean to. But if it was in self-defense, in a fight like that—well, that'll probably make a difference. But it's hard to say."

He opened the door of the house and waited for me to go in. "And it'll be hard for a jury too, don't you think?"

I nodded and went inside.

·16

O n Friday I only went to school in the morning. In the afternoon we went to Ed Maytubby's funeral, mostly because he was Maurice's uncle of course, although I guess Dad knew him pretty well even if I didn't.

I knew his son pretty well, for he was the same age as I was. Most of us called him Snake Maytubby, even though his real name was Carl, because Cecil Clelland always said that Maytubbys were Snake Indians.

Snake was sort of small and very quiet and gentle. At school he never did talk very much, although he was real friendly and smiled a lot. He had a funny laugh that made you want to laugh too when you heard him. He was a good basketball player even though he was short.

Once we were talking about hunting and things at lunch, and Snake told me that in the old days, in their tribe, when a hunter had killed a deer, he would take its head in his lap and whisper in its ear, "I have need, I have need," because they loved and respected the animal even though they killed it.

The funeral service was held at the grave-side, in a graveyard out near the Maytubby ranch. It was raining, and there was a sort of big canvas awning set up to keep the rain off both the casket and the family during the service. The rest of us stood around outside the shelter in the rain. It was really more a heavy mist than rain, but it was cold and uncomfortable all the same.

The funeral was kind of strange, because there were actually three services. First, there was a sort of religious ceremony under the awning, which was pretty short. When it was over, the coffin was opened, and everyone lined up and went past it and viewed the body.

I didn't really want to do that, but my folks were going past, so I went along too. I tried not to look at Mr. Maytubby, but I couldn't help it.

He was quite a bit older than Dad, but his hair was thick and black, without any gray in it, except for two real white streaks at the temples. You could hardly see the cut on his face.

After that there was an Indian ceremony, with some sort of chanting and singing in Indian. Then the casket was lowered into the open grave, which wasn't covered by the awning and was pretty muddy, and each member of the family put some kind of gift in the grave. I think they put some of his personal belongings in, too.

Then there was a military ceremony, because

once Mr. Maytubby had been in the army. Three men with soldiers' jackets and caps on fired a salute with old-looking rifles, and then someone played taps on a bugle.

I was watching Snake standing on the other side of the grave from me when the bugle started. He looked cold and sort of sick. And then he started to cry. Someone threw a shovelful of muddy dirt in on top of the casket, and Snake just stood there in the rain crying. I remembered the civet cats with the dirt in their nostrils.

I felt cold all the way home in the car. I asked Dad if the Maytubbys were Snake Indians, and he said he didn't know.

I thought of Carl standing there crying in the rain, and I wondered what I would say to him the next time I saw him at school.

·17

By the time we got home, the rain had stopped and the sky had started to clear. It was still cold, and I knew that everything would be soaked after four days of rain and snow. But I decided I simply had to go hunting that night. Imogene was coming to Billie Jean's the next day, so this was probably my last chance for several days, maybe even for a week.

It wasn't that I was just dying to go hunting. I still felt the cold from the afternoon at the cemetery. And I didn't seem to have the excitement I used to have about hunting any more. But Queenie and I had to get a coon. I knew that. With a really good coon hide, worth maybe $12.00 to $15.00, I thought we might have a chance to raise the money for Duke. I now had the money from my brother, and the possum hides I already had would soon be ready to sell, so one good coon hide would begin to make it look possible. Without it, we didn't have a chance.

I wondered if Duke had had a chance to go

hunting since we had shipped him back. I
hoped so.

I considered asking Maurice to go with me; I
knew I would like to have him for company,
especially if this turned out to be a long hunt.
But I decided against it. It wasn't a very good
night for pleasure hunting, and I didn't figure I
would be very good company tonight. Besides,
I sort of felt that I ought to do this myself. I
had started out to get Duke back myself, and
so far most of the money I had had been given
to me.

Dad came to my room after supper as I was
getting ready to go. "You wouldn't want me to
go with you tonight, Jess?" he said.

"No."

"I thought not," he said. He watched me put
on my mackinaw coat. "Have you got plenty of
matches and some dry twigs for a fire in case
you need one?"

"Yes."

"Going to take your rifle? You'll need it if
Queenie trees anything."

I'd thought about that, but I hadn't decided
yet. I looked out the window. It was twilight
now. Time to be going. I walked over to the
closet and put some shells in my jacket pocket.
Then I got my .22. It was a small rifle, but
now it felt big in my hand.

"Well, I guess I'll be going," I said.

We walked out into the yard. Queenie almost had an attack when she saw the rifle. Dad laughed and scratched her head when she slowed down once.

"Want a ride out to the woods?"

I said no.

"Well, good luck," he said. "Be careful."

Mother called good-bye from the back door as we left.

·18

Queenie really seemed ready for a hunt. The minute we entered the woods she was gone. It was dark now, and I couldn't see her once she was several feet away. I could hear her ranging about, running a little ways in one direction, then slowing to sniff more carefully for a minute, and then running on, only this time a little to one side, while she worked her way deeper into the woods all the time.

I followed along, going kind of slow, waiting for her to strike a trail. The leaves were wet and soggy underfoot, so the sounds we made were mostly muffled. I was glad there wasn't any wind.

It was about half an hour before Queenie hit a trail. By that time we were pretty far into the woods. I had just come to the bank of Cottonwood Creek when I heard her bay. She sounded a good ways off, but I couldn't tell how far. I stopped and listened. I wondered what sort of trail she was on, and whether it was a good one.

I knew the answer to that pretty soon. You

can tell by a dog's voice when it is on a really hot trail. And I could tell that that's what Queenie was on this time. I guess the smell of the animal must be so strong that the dog feels it's just about to catch it. And you know that the animal is not far in front of the dog, and that it's on the move, not somewhere holed up while the dog is following a trail made maybe half an hour ago.

I listened to Queenie for about five minutes, and began to feel excited. I was pretty sure that this was a coon, because Queenie was really on the move. If that had been a possum and her that hot on its trail, it would already have gone up a tree by now, and we would have had it.

But a coon's different. A coon's smart and tricky, and it's brave. I figured that if Queenie was on the trail of a coon I might as well find a good spot and make a fire and wait, for there wouldn't be any use following them. That coon would probably take them round and round in circles in this area before Queenie lost it and gave up, or else ran it up a tree.

I found a fairly level spot back up the slope from the creek bank and started to make a fire. All the time in the distance I could hear Queenie baying her excitement on the trail. I felt the old shiver of pleasure run down my back at the sound.

All the wood was wet, but with the dry twigs

I had brought I was able to get a fire going, and pretty soon some of the wood had dried out enough to give off a fair blaze. The warmth felt good. I sat down on a large rock over to one side. The flames cast shadows on the trees and rocks across the fire from me. I felt sort of strange sitting there. I couldn't help being excited at my first coon hunt by myself, and the loneliness made me feel good and bad at the same time. I wondered what would happen if Queenie managed to tree the coon. I looked at my .22 leaning up against a tree, with the fire reflecting off the barrel.

I got up and put another piece of wood on the fire. Then I turned up my coat collar and put my hands in my pockets. The log hissed as the fire turned the water to steam.

I could hear Queenie downstream now, still calling the trail. She hadn't lost it yet. I wondered whether she would be able to stay with the coon. Maybe it was a young one and wouldn't know so many tricks. An old coon would probably be too much for her.

The moon was up now, and scattered clouds drifted across it, so the trees almost seemed to move in the moonlight.

Once, several years earlier, my brother caught a young coon and brought it home for a pet. He kept it in a large cage he made for it, until it started acting real tame. Then he just left the cage open and let it come and go when it wanted to. It used its hands almost like a person. Pretty soon it could even open the screen door to the house. And every time you fed it, it would wash its food in its water bowl over and over. Dad said that was probably because of its instinct to wash the fish it would catch in a stream. With its small, delicate hands I thought it looked like a child washing its food.

The coon became quite tame, though it was something of a nuisance the way it came into the house almost any time it wanted to and the way it got into things. One of its favorite bits of mischief was to get into Mother's knitting basket and tangle up as much yarn as it could before she caught it. Mother would chase it out of the house with a broom, yelling like she was going to give it a real beating if she caught it. But once the coon was outside and we had got the yarn untangled and put back in the basket, I would see her smiling to herself or sometimes even chuckling out loud. And more often than not she would be out at its cage a few minutes later, making sure there was water and food.

But one day the coon left and never did come back. Dad said it probably went back to the woods to find a mate. We left its cage up for more than a week, hoping it would come back. Then Mother made my brother and me tear it down so that she wouldn't see it every time she looked out of the kitchen window, sitting there with its chicken-wire door hanging half open.

I got up and walked around the fire to stretch my legs. I stacked some wet branches near the fire to dry a bit and then stood with my back to the fire. It felt good after the damp rock. I could hear the creek down the hill from where I was. It was running higher than usual because of the last few days of rain. I tried to judge where Queenie was from her baying.

Dad once said that a tricky old coon could really give a hound fits when it got it near a stream. One of its tricks, he said, was to find a tree that leaned way out over the water and race up it and make a running jump to the other bank. Then the dog would find the trail stopped at the tree and think that the coon was treed, and it would stay there baying while the coon was getting away on the other side. It took a good hound to figure that one out.

They were coming back now. Queenie's voice was getting louder, and you could tell that she was coming almost straight back along the creek. I walked a little way down the hill toward the creek and stopped and listened. No doubt about it now. She was definitely on the other side of the creek. Somehow or other she had crossed over, probably swam, I thought. I felt sort of proud for Queenie. She hadn't let him lose her yet.

It was pretty cold away from the fire, so I went back and put more wood on it and stood looking toward the creek. Where I could see it in the moonlight, the water looked almost white.

Of course, a coon is good in the water. So the coon could have swum back across the creek already and left Queenie on the other side following a trail it had already backtracked on. I had heard Dad tell about that one, too. But I didn't think so. Queenie seemed too hot on his trail, so I didn't think he had had time to backtrack like that.

She was really close now. Unless they turned or something, she would be passing here any minute. I stepped around the fire and picked up my .22. The barrel felt cold and moist. I put it across my shoulder and walked down by the creek.

I saw Queenie pass through the trees on the other side, baying as she went. The creek was much louder here on the bank, but Queenie's voice was clear above the sound of the water. The trail was heading upstream now, and she was moving fast. I wondered whether I ought to go upstream too.

Not yet, I thought. No telling where they might go before it's over. So I walked back up to the fire. I leaned the rifle against a crack in the bark of a tree to keep it from falling. As I turned away, the moonlight caught the gun barrel, and just for a second it looked like the tail of a possum twisting on the ground in silence. I went over to the fire and sat down on the rock, with my back to the rifle, and tried not to think about it. I could almost feel it there behind me, standing up against the tree. I turned sideways to it, so that I could see it with one eye. It was better that way, though I still felt a little bit funny about it.

I could hear Queenie turning away now, moving almost straight away from me and the creek. The coon must be turning back into the woods now and leaving the creek bank. I wondered why.

One of the logs in the fire broke in the middle and fell into the bed of coals. It made a sharp crack and sent a little shower of sparks into the air. I jumped a bit at the sound.

The sky was almost all clear now, and I could see the stars overhead. I leaned back against a tree near the fire and thought about the night Imogene came out to find me beside the old Masonic Hall beneath the stars. The sky was dark and quiet. I couldn't even see her eyes. Queenie sounded a long ways off now. The fire felt warm and comfortable. I felt for my Barlow in my pocket and closed my eyes.

I don't know whether it was Queenie's barking
or the cold that woke me up. The fire had died
down to just a bed of coals, and my neck was
cold and stiff. Queenie sounded like she was
right in my lap, and I could tell that she had
treed.

The moon was real bright now, and I could
see her just below me beside the creek, looking
up into a tree and throwing back her head to
bay her loud call. Somehow they had crossed
the stream again, and she had treed the coon
pretty near to where the trail had started.

I got my flashlight and .22 and went down to
the tree. Queenie looked wet and tired, but she
was still bouncing around under the tree quite
a bit.

At first I thought she had made a false tree.
Even in the bright moonlight I couldn't see anything. I moved all the way around the base of
the tree twice before I finally saw it, and then
all I saw was one eye glinting in the flashlight
beam, right up against the main trunk of the

tree. Even then I wasn't sure because it went on and off almost like a light on an airplane. For a minute I thought maybe that's what I was seeing through the tree limbs.

Then I got a glimpse of its tail as I moved around trying for a better look. I could see what the coon was doing; it was moving around the tree with me but always keeping the tree trunk between us. It was a pretty good trick.

I held the flashlight under my arm while I put a shell in the .22. Then I shone the light in its eyes again, holding the flashlight up against the side of the rifle as I aimed it at the coon.

The best place to shoot is in the eye, or at least between the eyes, so that you don't damage the skin too much. But I couldn't tell where between the eyes was. The coon was on the dark side of the tree, so all I could see was the glint of the flashlight in its eye. I never did see both eyes at once.

I figured he was doing what Dad had told me about before, holding one paw over his eye and from time to time covering the other eye. I would have to shoot right at the eye, because I didn't know which side of the gleam to aim to. I could almost see his paw, small and delicate as a baby's hand, covering his eye from the light.

"Right in the eye, just like a squirrel," I heard Joe Hooker say. I held my breath and squeezed the trigger.

Queenie jumped toward the tree at the sound of the rifle, and I saw splinters of bark fly into the light beam. Then I saw the coon sailing through the air toward the creek. He was right side up, and he had his feet spread as if he had jumped for the water. If he was hurt, it wasn't very bad.

He hit the water, and Queenie left the bank at about the same time. For a few seconds they were both under water, and all I could hear was the sound of the water rushing along the creek. Then I saw the coon's head bob to the surface, and a second later Queenie's head and shoulders surfaced about a foot downstream from him. Then they went behind a tree as they swept downstream.

I ran downstream a little ways to an open place and stood on the lip of the bank. Now I could see them coming into sight, Queenie heaving and pawing at the water and the coon perched right on her neck and shoulders and forcing her head down into the water. This was one trick I hadn't thought about, and I stood there shocked at the sight of the coon drowning Queenie.

Queenie was a good fighter and a powerful dog, and I knew it. On dry land that coon would have been no match for her. But in the water I could see that he had the advantage. Once or twice Queenie managed to heave her head above the surface, but the coon just hung on and pushed her head right back into the swirling water.

I really didn't think about what I was doing. Suddenly I just jumped off the bank into the creek. The water rose up above my waist right at the edge, and it felt like I had just had all the breath knocked out of me, it was so cold. I grabbed a bush sticking out of the bank with one hand to keep from being washed off my feet, and as Queenie and the coon came past me I swung my rifle butt at the coon's head as hard as I could.

I felt the jar all the way up my arm when it hit, and the rifle barrel was almost knocked out of my hand. It made a dull, soggy sort of sound when it hit.

I saw Queenie come up gasping and snorting and start for the bank, and then I turned around and pulled myself back up onto the bank too. I laid the rifle down on the ground and went over to help Queenie.

Then I saw the body of the coon, caught for a minute by the root of a tree, and I leaned down and pulled it out of the water. It was soft in my hands, and the water ran down from it in little pools at my feet.

I was so wet and cold that I felt like my legs had turned to water. I could hardly stand up, and I was beginning to shake pretty bad.

I laid the coon down on the bank and started up the slope toward the fire. Queenie was still shaking herself and snorting right beside the creek.

There was still a good bed of coals from the fire, but I was beginning to think I would freeze before I got the fire kindled up again enough to help. I took off my shoes and pants and laid them across some rocks beside the fire to dry. My bare legs and feet felt almost numb from the cold, but it was better than feeling like they were wrapped up in ice packs. I sat as close to the fire as I could get without scorching. Queenie came over and sat beside me, and I stroked her head. Then, as wet as she was, she went to sleep. She just sort of slid down alongside the rock and came to a stop with her head resting on my foot.

After a while I went down by the creek and got the coon and brought it up by the fire. I laid it down on a rock near where I had been sitting. Queenie didn't even stir.

I stood in the cold and looked at it. There was a little blood oozing out of its nostrils, and its eyes were about half open. They looked dull and smokey. I reached out to touch the dark band of hair around the face, and my fingers touched the side of its head. It was soft and mushy, like Ladd's. I felt tired and cold and sick. "I have need," I whispered. "I have need."

And suddenly I started to cry. I just stood there in the moonlight like Carl Maytubby and cried.

·20

It was daylight by the time I got home. Dad was just about ready to start out looking for me. Mother was in the kitchen fixing him a thermos of coffee when I came inside. She turned around and hugged me, and she was smiling. But I could tell she had been crying.

She said for me to get right to bed, and I said that's just what I wanted to do. All the time I was taking off my coat she kept fussing and saying how I needed to get warm and to sleep, just as if she needed to talk me into it.

Dad asked me if I wanted him to skin the coon, and I told him to wait until I woke up. He looked at me sort of surprised like for a minute. Then he said O.K.

I didn't wake up until almost 4 o'clock in the afternoon and even then I didn't feel like getting up yet. I just lay there in bed, looking at the ceiling. The covers sort of pushed me down, warm and comfortable. I tried to go back to sleep, but I knew I had to do something about the coon.

Pretty soon I got up and dressed and got something to eat. Mother wanted to know how I felt, and I said just fine. She said it was a wonder I didn't catch pneumonia, staying out in the cold all night like that.

When I finished eating, I went out to the garage where Dad had put the coon. It was lying on a work table on its side, with the tail hanging off the edge, sort of the way you might see one hanging over the side of a tree limb. Even in the dim light of the garage the tail looked beautiful, with the black rings against the reddish-brown of the rest of the fur.

"It's a fine coon," Dad said, as he came up behind me. "One of the best I've ever seen. I guess you feel pretty proud about it."

I shook my head, and he said, "I'm surprised Queenie could still tree a coon like that."

I took the coon and a drying-board and went around beside the garage. The sun was pretty low now and didn't give off much heat. Queenie was lying up against the wall in the sun. She wagged her tail as I came over, but she didn't get up.

"How much do you think he might be worth?" Dad said.

I laid the coon on the ground and knelt beside him, feeling his fur with my hands.

"I don't know," I said.

I could tell he was a big coon, as Dad had

said, and there were no holes in the fur. But he looked small lying there in front of me, with the dirt and dried blood at the sides of his nostrils. I kept remembering how his head had felt when I had touched it. I didn't touch it now.

I took out my Barlow and whetted it on the side of my shoe. Dad said he'd be back in a few minutes and went into the house.

I took one of the coon's feet in my hand and turned him over on his back. The paw was black and smooth inside when I opened the toes, and the pads of the individual joints looked fat and soft and tender. They looked almost too small to support him. I wondered what he was worth, what he was really worth.

And I wondered what Duke was worth, and also what he cost. Certainly the $50.00 was the least of it. "Maybe he costs too much," Imogene had said. "Unquote," I thought. I didn't feel like smiling.

Once again I remembered how Duke had looked when we shipped him back to Kentucky, cold and miserable and scared. I wanted it to be better for him than that. I wanted him to be happy and eager to hunt—somewhere. But at least he was still alive.

The coon lay at my feet in the dry winter grass.

I snapped the blade of my Barlow and put it in my pocket. Then I carried the coon and the drying-board back into the garage. As I came out of the garage, dad came out of the house again and stood there waiting as I walked back to the house.

"Finished?" he said.

I shook my head no. "I'm not going to skin him," I said. "Tomorrow's Sunday. I'll take him back to the woods tomorrow and bury him there."

"It's a nice coon," Dad said. "Probably worth $15.00. It'll be hard for you to get enough money for Duke if you don't sell this hide."

"I know," I said. "But I don't think I'm going to be doing so much hunting that I'll need another hunting dog now." I tried not to think what mother could do with an extra $15.00.

Dad nodded a little, and we went inside to supper.

·21

After supper I went over to Billie Jean's house. I had decided I would invite Imogene out for a soda or something, now that I wasn't going to be spending the money on a dog. But I didn't feel very cheered up by the idea.

Imogene answered the door herself. I hadn't quite expected that, and it took me by surprise. She had on a pale yellow blouse, and her hair was hanging loose around her face. She was smiling like she was real happy to see me. I felt almost like I did when I jumped into the water, for it made me catch my breath. I was barely able to ask her out for a soda.

We went inside to tell Billie Jean's mother that we were going downtown, and Imogene went to get her coat. I talked to Billie Jean's brother Jim while I waited.

"When are you going to be getting your dog back?" he said.

Imogene came back into the room then, and we walked to the door. I helped her put on her coat.

"I'm not going to," I said. "I finally decided he costs too much."

I opened the door, and we stepped outside. The wind was up a bit now, and it felt cold. It was at our backs as we headed downtown. I shivered a little and turned up my coat collar.

Somewhere across town I heard a dog howling. I looked over at Imogene but didn't say anything. She smiled in the moonlight and touched my arm with her hand.